BY GITTY DANESHVARI

ILLUSTRATED BY JAMES LANCETT

LITTLE, BROWN BOOKS FOR YOUNG READERS
www.lbkids.co.uk

LITTLE, BROWN BOOKS FOR YOUNG READERS

First published in the US in 2015 by Little, Brown and Company
First published in the UK in 2015 by Hodder & Stoughton

1 3 5 7 9 10 8 6 4 2

A CIP catalogue record for this book
is available from the British Library.

ISBN 978-0-349-12420-9

Printed and bound by CPI Group (UK) Ltd, Croydon, CR0 4YY

The paper and board used in this book are made from
wood from responsible sources.

MIX
Paper from
responsible sources
FSC® C104740

Little, Brown Books for Young Readers
An imprint of
Hachette Children's Group
Part of Hodder & Stoughton
Carmelite House
50 Victoria Embankment
London EC4Y 0DZ

An Hachette UK Company
www.hachette.co.uk

www.lbkids.co.uk

For the always exceptional Bee,
aka Isobel Rose Smythe.
Here's to many adventures to come.

TOP SECRET

"When people say that 'the children are the future,' they aren't talking about me."

—Jonathan Murray, 12,
Evanston, Virginia

SECURE DOCUMENTS

CHAPTER 1

<098762-JM-LOUC-101>

Ordinary. Normal. Average. Unexceptional.

Awful words: the whole lot of them. Why, just saying them can turn a mouth sour! An exaggeration? Absolutely not. To be an ordinary, normal, average, unexceptional child in a world that celebrates *first place, the best, top of the class,* and so on is tantamount to being invisible. It's the human equivalent of wallpaper, someone who just blends into the background. So who would have ever imagined that two ordinary, normal, average, and highly unexceptional children would be tasked with saving the country after the greatest security breach in history?

OCTOBER 14, 7:45 A.M. MCLEAN, VIRGINIA

"There is no way a trained seal could do my job!" Arthur Pelton huffed at his wife, Franny, while fastening the shiny brass buckles on his uniform. A size too small, the navy-blue suit covered Arthur's meatball-esque figure so tightly that it cut off a significant amount of oxygen to his extremities, leaving his face, hands, and feet perpetually pink and puffy.

"A trained orangutan or a monkey, *maybe*. But a seal? Never!" Arthur continued as he furrowed his brow with frustration.

"You sit on a stool and point at a sign all day. I'm pretty sure a seal could do that," Franny replied, stifling a yawn.

"Seals have flippers, not fingers. They couldn't point even if they wanted to. And believe me, they don't want to!" Arthur shouted as he stormed out the front door.

Whether from anger or the physical exertion of slamming the door, Arthur had to pause on the front stoop to wipe his perspiring brow. His stubby little fingers scooped the sweat from his forehead and smoothed it across his thinning salt-and-pepper locks. Not that he was thinking about his thinning hair or propensity for perspiration. Arthur was still stuck on seals. How *did* he know seals didn't want to point? Maybe they did. And now that he thought of it, they could *motion* toward the sign, which was kind of like pointing. Franny was right. A seal *could* do his job.

Arthur's face dropped; his jowls sagged and his eyes closed. Total devastation. But then a smile slowly emerged as he reviewed the basics of his job. He worked the guard booth at an out-of-use delivery gate. But he didn't *just point* at the sign in the window, which stated that the gate was "no longer in service," any time a car or person approached. *He also sat on a stool.* How would the seal get onto the stool? Seals can't climb. They don't even have legs!

Arthur was not an intelligent man. Reading the ingredients on a box of crackers exhausted him. Counting was an activity that still required the use of his fingers. Needless to say, it was nothing short of a miracle that Arthur had a job. And not just any job, but a job protecting the president of the United

States of America. Or so he claimed. In reality a cavalry of highly trained Secret Service agents protected the president, and Arthur manned a defunct delivery gate located on the west side of the White House.

OCTOBER 14, 11:07 A.M. THE WHITE HOUSE. WASHINGTON, DC

"Excuse me." A steely yet high-pitched voice jolted Arthur from what appeared to be a nap.

"I wasn't sleeping! I just have really bad posture!" Arthur blurted out as he turned toward the voice.

Standing at the booth's window in oversized sunglasses, a trench coat with the collar turned up, and a baseball cap was a *very* tiny man. So tiny that Arthur couldn't help but wonder if he was tall enough to ride a roller coaster. Or drive a car. Surely he couldn't see over the wheel. *Unless, of course, he has a specially equipped car*, Arthur mused as the short-statured man stared at him. At least Arthur assumed he was staring at him. It was rather hard to tell where the man's eyes were focused behind his baseball cap and sunglasses.

Arthur nodded his head ever so slightly as he

mulled over a new idea. "Have you just come from the eye doctor? Because they're not supposed to let you leave unless someone picks you up. You probably can't see a thing. Do you even know where you are?"

The small man stood completely still as he continued to look in Arthur's general direction.

"*I said*, do you know where you are?" Arthur repeated in a slow and deliberate fashion, all the while clenching his jaw. "Oh, I get it: Mr. Important doesn't want to talk to a boring old security guard. What are you, some kind of really short celebrity? Man, do I hate celebrities! I remember this one time—"

The tiny man interrupted, "I am not a *really short celebrity*. And to answer your question, yes, I know where I am, Mr. Pelton."

Arthur paused.

He opened his mouth.

He closed his mouth.

He narrowed his eyes.

"How do you know my name?"

"This, Mr. Pelton, is my house. I know everyone's names."

"Man, you are *seriously* lost. This is the White House, like where the president lives," Arthur answered with a smirk, motioning toward the large white structure behind him.

"Mr. Pelton, I am with the Secret Service. Or rather, I *run* the Secret Service, which means I run the White House, which means this is my house."

Arthur shrugged. "I guess that's kind of true...."

"The truth doesn't come in *kind of*s, Mr. Pelton. Things are either true or false. Those are the only options," the tiny man barked. "Moving on, I am here today because the Secret Service needs your help."

"I'm in!" Arthur squealed before even hearing what the man had in mind.

"We will be conducting a training mission tonight at nineteen hundred hours. And as such, we will require your assistance in accessing the west perimeter of the White House."

"Nineteen hundred hours," Arthur repeated as he counted on his fingers.

"Seven p.m., Mr. Pelton. Nineteen hundred hours is also known as seven p.m."

"I knew that."

Arthur Pelton most definitely did not know that.

"Until tonight," the tiny man said, and then turned to leave. "Oh, and, Mr. Pelton, they don't call us the *Secret* Service for nothing. You are not to tell a soul about this. Not. One. Soul."

OCTOBER 14, 6:57 P.M. THE WHITE HOUSE, WASHINGTON, DC

A heavy fog hung low over the capital, obscuring the tops of trees and a large portion of the district's monuments. The soft sound of classical music emanated from the White House. Arthur stuffed tissues in his ears as he bemoaned the yearly visit of the Metropolitan Children's Philharmonic, currently playing for an audience that included the president, the vice president, and the secretary of state.

Tap, tap, tap.

Arthur yelped (of course he did; that's what his wife, Franny, would have said).

The short-statured man from the Secret Service, whose face was once again obscured by a baseball cap, stood at the booth's window.

"I had to put tissues in my ears because of the—"

"The Met Chil Phil. They're nothing but a bunch of ingrates," the man interrupted. "Now on to business." He then pointed to the gate, followed by a keypad on the wall next to Arthur. But Arthur didn't move. He just sat there, utterly paralyzed. He had never opened the gate; it had been out of service long before he had even started working at the White House.

"Mr. Pelton," the man from the Secret Service said as sweat dripped steadily from Arthur's brow.

This was his big moment, Arthur's one chance to shine. And yet he couldn't remember the code, which had been given to him on the off chance that an emergency might warrant opening the gate.

The small man's voice grew louder, cutting sharply through the brisk air. "Is there a problem, Mr. Pelton?"

And then, as if by magic, Arthur remembered the code, punched in the numbers, and smiled excitedly.

"Good luck—or do you guys not say that in your business? How about knock 'em dead? Or break a leg?" Arthur babbled, prompting the man to twirl his hand dramatically in the air.

"What's that about? You pretending to be one of those fancy guys who waves a stick at musicians?" Arthur grumbled as the man from the Secret Service disappeared into the night.

Within hours, the vice president of the United States had been kidnapped. The nation's greatest group of spies deactivated. And one of two codes necessary to access the government's mainframe, which housed classified documents belonging to the White House, the Department of Justice, the FBI, and the CIA, had been stolen. And all because Arthur Pelton wanted to prove that he wasn't just some nobody doing a job that even a trained seal could handle.

TOP SECRET

"How dare you say I'm *under*performing!? Everyone knows that the real problem is that the others are *over*performing!"

—Sally Jenkins, 11,
Little Rock, Arkansas

SECURE DOCUMENTS

CHAPTER 2

<099366-SJ-LOUC-148>

There's an old adage that everyone has a story. However, nowhere does it say that everyone has an *interesting* story. Twelve-year-old Jonathan Murray did *not* have an interesting story. And he knew it. Every morning he looked in the mirror and thought, *This is it. This is what I'm stuck with.* He was average, middle-of-the-road, and pedestrian in every way that the world deemed relevant— academically, athletically, socially, and so on. Even his appearance—nondescript black hair that clung to his forehead as if it were in danger of falling off and thick eyebrows—was utterly normal, neither attractive nor unattractive. But none of this surprised Jonathan, for long ago, or as long ago as a twelve-year-old can remember, he had accepted his fate. Nothing was ever going to change. Or so he thought.

OCTOBER 15, 6:58 A.M. EVANSTON, VIRGINIA

It was fast approaching seven a.m. and the sky was still a dull gray. Rain clouds lingered in the distance. The sun, heavily muted, cast a dim, almost candle-like light. Shadows lurked about the ground, crawling from one house to the next. It was quiet. Not even a bird chirped. This was not by accident, but rather due to Evanston's city ordinance on irksome sounds—officially called "noise pollution"—which included everything from chirpy birds to whistling in the street to poorly tuned cars. Of course, regulating birds was nowhere near as easy as regulating cars and people who whistled, but Evanston's Community Patrol found a way. *They always found a way.* And in this particular case "finding a way" meant introducing laryngitis to the bird population, leaving them incapable of chirping any louder than a whisper.

Located just across the Potomac River from Washington, DC, Evanston was well known for its precision. Gardeners regularly measured grass strands to maintain uniform lawn heights. Sprinklers ran counterclockwise at eight a.m. and clockwise at nine p.m. It was a town of doers, of overachievers, of goal-oriented people. Parents groomed children from birth to excel not only academically but athletically, musically, linguistically, philanthropically, extracurricularly, and so on. It was for this reason that 98.5 percent of Evanston High School's last graduating class went on to Ivy League universities. The remaining 1.5 percent fled abroad to avoid bringing further shame to their families. Bottom line: Evanston was an uptight town.

So it was quite a surprise—a shock really—when on the morning of October 15 at 6:58 a.m., a garbage truck sputtered and clunked (a direct violation of the city's noise ordinance) down Forrester Lane. It stopped in front of number sixteen, the lone eyesore on the block. Broken-down bicycles littered the lawn. The once white picket fence was now gray and pretty much picket-less. The house was painted half yellow and half green, not by design, but rather laziness. That's right, the inhabitants had lost interest in their home improvement project halfway through, stopping without even bothering to put away the ladder, bucket, or paintbrush. Pinned to the front door was a wad of fading notices from Evanston's Community Patrol asking the inhabitants to *please* tidy up or else they would have no choice but to leave *another note*. (Full disclosure: Evanston's Community Patrol was an all-volunteer group with no legal standing.)

Sleeping soundly, tucked beneath plain white sheets, in his room on the second story of number sixteen Forrester Lane was Jonathan Murray. It was a dreary room with little in the way of personal items. A calendar from the local dry cleaner hung over the bed. The thick shag carpet, while clean, was a drab shade of brown that matched the curtains. The bedside table contained an old alarm clock and a hairbrush, nothing more. And it was here, amid this dowdy decor, that Jonathan suddenly awoke and cocked his head to the left, much like a dog whose owner had called his name. He then pushed back the sheets, walked to the window, and sighed. Jonathan was always sighing, a result of finding himself terribly dull.

There was a garbage truck idling in front of the house. Only it wasn't trash day, Jonathan thought, and while the truck looked like one of Evanston's eco-friendly fleet, it didn't sound like it. Curious, Jonathan leaned out his bedroom window and squinted down at the street. A camera with a tele-photo lens was hanging out the passenger-side window snapping pictures. Why would anyone want photographs of his house, Jonathan wondered, until the appearance of a bicycle with a billowing red flag distracted him. On the bike was a Community Patrol volunteer, eager to write up the driver for both noise pollution and trash day schedule violation. However, upon seeing the bicyclist, the driver immediately put the truck in gear and clunked away.

Never one to give up issuing a ticket without a fight, the Community Patrol volunteer popped a flashing red light on the handlebars and set off in pursuit. Still standing at the window, Jonathan turned his attention to Freddy the paperboy, who was tiptoeing up his neighbors' driveway, carefully

laying the *Washington Chronicle* on the doorstep. Unlike other mornings, Freddy paused and then carefully inspected the front page. Although Jonathan couldn't see what had piqued Freddy's interest, he would later learn it was a photo of a wild-eyed man with a six-inch gray Afro shoving a cookie into his mouth, alongside the headline: "Real-Life Cookie Monster Faces 100 Years in Jail."

The sound of giggling, Jonathan's parents' giggling to be precise, drifted into his room, reminding him that it was a school day. Jonathan then showered, put on his standard outfit of khakis and a sensible sweater, and headed down to the kitchen. Posters of rock bands lined the hallway, each taped or pinned haphazardly, keeping them consistently crooked. At the foot of the stairs, an arcade-sized Pac-Man game and a popcorn machine framed the entryway to the kitchen, aka the comic book library. There were literally stacks of old editions stored in the oven, freezer, and pantry.

"There he is! Our favorite child!" Mickey Murray called out as Jonathan entered the kitchen.

Mickey had the appearance of a skateboarder or a surfer, with blond windswept hair, a honey-colored tan, and a getup that included both swim shorts and sandals.

"Well, if it isn't our number one son!" dark-haired and olive-skinned Carmen Murray hollered in her thick Mexican accent, pumping her arms in the air as if performing a well-orchestrated routine.

Petite and smiley, Carmen still bore a striking resemblance, both physically and mentally, to the cheerleader she had once been. And while Jonathan liked cheerleaders well enough, he sometimes found his mother's optimistic approach to life bordering on delusional.

"I don't mean to sound ungrateful, but being 'number one' or your 'favorite' child isn't much of an accomplishment when there's only one kid. I mean, there's not even a *dog* to compete against," Jonathan grumbled as he picked up empty bags of chips and tossed them into the trash can.

"You want a dog? I can get you a dog. Old Lady Preston can't even remember how many she has; we can take one off her hands *easily*," Mickey declared confidently.

"Dad, petnapping is illegal," Jonathan muttered, and then sighed. "Why are you guys up so early?"

"All-night horror fest on channel 563. It was awesome. Zombies, zombies, and more zombies," Mickey said, and then swigged a big gulp of milk straight from the carton.

"Hey," Carmen said as she tapped Mickey's arm. "What did I say about the milk?"

"To leave some for you. My bad, babe."

"It's all good," Carmen said with a wink as Jonathan inwardly cringed.

Why did his mom and dad feel the need to talk like this? The other parents in Evanston didn't use expressions like "it's all good" and "my bad." No, the other mothers and fathers were adults, and as such they peppered their speech with dignified phrases like "to the best of my knowledge" and "with all due respect."

Jonathan grabbed his lunch from the refrigerator and halfheartedly waved good-bye to his parents. "Well, I'm off to school."

"Not so fast. We need to talk about that report card," Carmen said in a serious tone. "Way!! To!! Go!!!"

"Mom, I got straight Cs."

"And we're darn proud of you for it," Mickey said, saluting his son.

"You guys really need to raise your standards," Jonathan moaned. "I'm pretty sure this is how you wound up at a university whose acceptance policy consists of dialing a 1-800 number."

Mickey and Carmen Murray were fine and decent people. They just happened to have never really grown up; they were stranded at sixteen— permanently. They thought that dog walking was a career. They never voted. They *sort of* paid taxes. They referred to Max Arons, the president of the United States, as the Boss Man because they couldn't remember his name. They did their grocery shopping at 7-Eleven. But they loved their son. And that was all that mattered, according to a fortune cookie they once read.

Jonathan pulled on his backpack and exited the house at exactly 8:15 a.m., the time when all Evanstonian students were encouraged by the Community Patrol to depart so as to avoid tardiness. Jonathan nodded hello to his neighbor's ancient pug, sunbathing on the lawn, and then turned onto the sidewalk next to a tall, athletic boy in a letterman jacket.

"Good morning, Tom," Jonathan offered flatly.

"Oh, hey! You must be that new kid my mom was telling me about. Welcome to Evanston. You're going to love it here. Especially if you play ice hockey, number one in the nation four years running," Tom said, and then pointed to one of many shiny gold pins on his jacket.

Jonathan brushed away the hair on his forehead and rolled his eyes. Some things never changed. "Tom, it's me, Jonathan Murray. We've lived three doors down from each other our whole lives. Your sister Cathy once babysat me. It was kind of a big deal. She lost me at the mall and then took home some other kid because she couldn't remember what I looked like."

"No way! That was you? Crazy! Well, see you around, Jeff," Tom replied, and then disappeared into the herd of students crowding the sidewalk.

This was the story of Jonathan's life. No one ever noticed him, so he could hardly be surprised when they failed to remember him. He was white rice, there but never focused on. And yet as Jonathan puttered along at the tail end of the mass of students, he heard footsteps behind him. Steps that mimicked his own, starting and stopping just as Jonathan did. He shook his head, certain that it was a case of mistaken identity. For no one would ever *purposely* follow Jonathan Murray. Eager to educate the misguided stalker, Jonathan turned around and scanned the street behind him. But there wasn't a soul in sight.

And so the boy continued on his way, unnerved by the sensation that someone was watching him, paying attention to his every move.

"My child is NOT an honor student at Fairfax Middle School, nor does he plan on being one at Fairfax High School."

—Mrs. Margaret Hardin, 40, Vienna, Virginia

CHAPTER 3

OCTOBER 15, 8:26 A.M. EVANSTON MIDDLE
SCHOOL. EVANSTON, VIRGINIA

The quad at Evanston Middle School consisted of
perfectly trimmed grass surrounded by redbrick
buildings, cleaned biweekly so as to maintain their
rich color. Classical music played in the halls, and
organic food carts filled the cafeteria. To put it simply, Evanston Middle School took being the best
very seriously.

A small-framed girl with shoulder-length dirty-
blond hair, round glasses, and slightly hunched

shoulders made her way across the student-filled quad.

"Hey, Sarah," the girl offered with a smile, but Sarah didn't so much as glance in her direction.

"What's up, Phil? You chillin' like a villain?" the girl called out cheerfully as she continued across the grass, having failed to elicit even the faintest response from the boy. "Just kidding, you are obviously *not* a villain. But that's not to say you aren't strong and tough like a villain. I guess the real question is, do you want to be a villain? You know what? I'd like to retract that whole comment. Forget I said a word. Talk soon!"

It would be easy to assume that Sarah and Phil were ignoring the girl on purpose, but that simply wasn't the case. The girl's name was Shelley Brown. And to put it bluntly, she was forgettable. She had a face that looked like a million other faces. Brown eyes. Smallish nose. Normal-sized ears. And then there was her voice. Shelley was cursed with a soft voice, one that merged with surrounding sounds and further hindered her quest to be noticed. So terrible was Shelley's vocal affliction that she once sang the entire national anthem in front of her history class without anyone even noticing.

Twelve-year-old Shelley was the younger of two girls born to world-renowned scientists Dr. Heathcliff Brown and his wife, Dr. Lillian Brown. The Browns had relocated to Germany four years prior to run a research lab. However, Shelley had been unable to learn German from YouTube videos as the rest of her highly academic family had, and so she was sent to live with her maternal grandparents in Evanston, Virginia.

"Remember, Shells, life is a bowl of cherries... or was it cherubs? A bowl of small, plump babies or fruit? Neither really makes sense. Why can I never remember these things?" Shelley mumbled to herself as she entered one of the brick buildings off the quad, annoyed that she couldn't even get her own pep talk right.

Shelley took her usual seat in American Government and then turned to the boy next to her. "Hey, Gavin, you ready to watch the president's State of the Union address, also known as a really long speech from the leader of the free world? Although,

I don't know if that's still accurate. I mean, aren't corporations the new leaders of the free world?"

Gavin stared straight ahead, unaware that anyone was even speaking to him. Unfazed, Shelley leaned over and tapped the boy on the arm. "Hey!"

Gavin turned and looked Shelley straight in the eyes. "That's not your seat."

"Mr. Apted moved me here about three weeks ago. Remember, I let you cheat off me on the last test? And for that I should really apologize. I had no business letting you think that I was smart. I know that I look like a nerd, but I don't have the brain of one. Talk about false advertising!" Shelley said, lifting her eyebrows. "But we're all good, right, Gav?"

Staring at Shelley, carefully taking in her nondescript face, Gavin asked, "Who are you?"

"Shelley. Shelley Brown. But feel free to call me Samantha."

"Samantha?" Gavin repeated with a perplexed look.

"That's what you called me a week ago. And honestly, I've always liked the name. So really, I should thank you, Gav!"

"Okay...whatever," Gavin said as he turned away.

In that moment, Shelley knew the conversation was being erased from Gavin's memory. It's what people did. They let go of pointless, meaningless interactions in order to make room for the worthwhile ones. And sadly, for reasons Shelley could never understand, she wasn't regarded as a girl of substance, a girl to be listened to, a girl worth remembering.

As the president spoke to the nation, Shelley's attention drifted from the television to her classmates, none of whom she could call friends. They were strangers even after four years in Evanston. Her eyes bounced from face to face until finally landing on the window to the corridor. It was then that she noticed a woman, but not just any woman: Nurse Maidenkirk. Tall with flame-red hair and lips thinner than thread, she was clad in a sharply ironed white dress that came just below the knees, pale stockings, thick wedged shoes, and a small square hat with a red cross on it. And though Nurse Maidenkirk looked as she always did, there was

something about the way she stared at Shelley now that sent a chill up the young girl's spine.

Two corridors away, a hall monitor entered Mr. Dunlap's Spanish class and handed him an official-looking slip.

"I'm sorry, young man, but there's no Jonathan Murray in this class," Mr. Dunlap said.

Jonathan sighed and then quickly stood up. "I'm Jonathan Murray."

Mr. Dunlap stared at the boy suspiciously.

"And no, I'm not new," Jonathan answered as though for the thousandth time.

"Well, of course you aren't new. I know that," Mr. Dunlap poorly covered. "But has your name always been Jonathan? Because I'm pretty sure it used to be Hank—or was it Salvador?"

"Jonathan. It's always been Jonathan Murray."

"Well, '*Jonathan*,' " Mr. Dunlap said, using his fingers to mimic quotation marks, "Nurse Maidenkirk wants to see you."

Great, Jonathan thought as he made his way down the hall toward the infirmary. The last time he saw Nurse Maidenkirk, she had regaled him with gory stories about the gruesome practices used in the early days of medicine before pinning him to the bed and jabbing his arm with a needle. Failing to get a flu shot was tantamount to spreading smallpox in Evanston, and so the Community Patrol had asked Nurse Maidenkirk to take matters into her own hands where resisters were concerned.

Jonathan entered the stark white lobby of the infirmary and began looking around.

"Mr. Murray," Nurse Maidenkirk hissed as she

approached, a large needle in her left hand. "Did you hear the Feldmans' cat was hit by a car this morning? It survived, but apparently it left quite a stain on the road."

A word Jonathan had learned the month before in English class suddenly popped into his mind: *macabre*. It meant horrifying, gruesome, or ghastly.

"That's really sad. Poor cat," Jonathan mumbled, his eyes glued to the sharp metal tip of the needle in Nurse Maidenkirk's hand. "I'm pretty sure I'm up to date on my vaccinations if that's what this is about."

Nurse Maidenkirk pressed the tip of the syringe, sending a few drops of clear liquid straight into the air. "Very well, then."

The flame-haired woman dropped the needle into the front pocket of her dress, adjusted her small white cap, and then motioned for Jonathan to follow her into the next room.

Twelve hospital beds, each with its own private curtain, lined the walls of the sick bay. Metallic fixtures with flickering lightbulbs hung from the ceiling. And an old television, half the size of a Buick, sat atop a cart on the far side of the room.

"Nurse Maidenkirk, what am I doing here?" Jonathan asked, his arms tightly crossed.

"The Feldmans estimate the car was moving ten miles an hour. Imagine what would have happened if it had been going faster," Nurse Maidenkirk said, having completely ignored Jonathan's question.

"Thanks, but I'd rather not."

"As you wish," Nurse Maidenkirk said as she turned to leave.

"Where are you going?"

"Why? Did you wish to discuss the Feldmans' cat further? I suppose we could review the damage done to the feline's spleen."

"I'm not really interested in the cat's spleen. Can't I just leave?" Jonathan asked.

"No, you can't." And with that, Nurse Maidenkirk exited the sick bay.

From the far corner of the room came the sound of a door creaking open. Jonathan stepped closer. A girl—small, with dirty-blond hair and brown eyes—exited the bathroom.

"Jerome?" "Susan?" Shelley and Jonathan blurted out simultaneously.

But before either could correct the other, one

of the crisp white hospital curtains whipped open, revealing a tall and lanky man in his mid-forties. His jet-black hair was heavily oiled and carefully arranged, his part so straight, it might have been done with a ruler. Dressed in a gray double-breasted suit with a thin black tie and well-polished oxfords, he looked positively out of place in the school's infirmary, not to mention this decade.

"That's the thing about you unexceptionals, you don't even remember each other," the man said in a quick, rapid-fire manner before popping a toothpick into his mouth.

"The name's Hammett, with two *t*s. Hammett Humphries," the man added in a gravelly tone that reminded both Jonathan and Shelley of someone overcoming a bout of the flu.

Hammett quickly sized up the kids, scanning everything from their shoes to the hair on their heads, all the while bouncing the toothpick from side to side in his mouth.

"Listen up, kiddos, 'cause I don't have time to say this twice. Well, actually I do, I just don't have the patience—"

"Is this about my art project? Because I realize

it was a little...how should I say...avant-garde—"
Shelley started to explain.

"Enough with the chitchat, kid. I'm not here about some weird-looking papier-mâché thing. I've got news. Big news. The kind of news that will turn your socks inside out."

"You've got big news for *me*? Jonathan Murray of sixteen Forrester Lane?" the boy asked skeptically.

"That's right, kid. I've got big news for both of you," Hammett announced, tossing his toothpick into the trash can and then promptly popping in a new one.

"Well, what is it?" Jonathan inquired.

"From the moment these words leave my lips, nothing's going to be the same. Not a doggone thing. You understand?"

"No offense, but I don't really believe that. Unless, of course, you tell me that you poisoned me ten minutes ago. But how could you have poisoned me ten minutes ago if we just met?" Shelley rambled.

"Listen, doll, you don't have to believe me, but the truth is simple. After I tell you, you're not going to see the world the same way. You're not even going to see *yourself* the same way."

"Just tell Hammett you believe him," Jonathan mumbled to Shelley, eager to get to the point of all this commotion.

"Okay, fine, we're never going to be the same," Shelley relented.

Hammett nodded, widened his eyes, and took a deep breath. The kids watched the man with bubbling impatience. Shelley pursed her lips to stop herself from yelling, "Oh just get on with it!" And then right as Jonathan was about to release a sigh fraught with frustration, Hammett looked them both straight in the eyes. But this wasn't just any old look. It was a heavy, burdensome expression, one that made Hammett appear at least a decade older.

"Are you telling us telepathically? You know, brain to brain? Because I've been told I have something of a gift in the supernatural realm," Shelley said, while Jonathan rolled his eyes.

Unwilling to let Shelley derail the moment, Hammett pressed on. "The League of Unexceptional Children needs you, both of you," he declared dramatically, thrusting a pointer finger in each of the kids' faces.

Jonathan nodded to be polite, but he hadn't a clue what Hammett was talking about. Not one clue.

"Is that the bowling team for uncoordinated kids?" Shelley asked before breaking into a confident smile. "I knew I'd get a callback! Silver fingers and sticky feet equal dynamo in the lanes!"

"I don't understand what silver fingers even means. Do you wear silver gloves?" Jonathan asked Shelley, while Hammett started shaking his head.

"Our country is in grave danger and we're just about out of hope," Hammett blustered in a way that only a frustrated adult could. "Except for you two, that is…"

"So you're definitely not a bowler?" Shelley interjected, pushing her glasses up the bridge of her nose.

"We're not bowlers, kid," Hammett said, bending down until he was mere inches from Shelley's face. "We're spies."

"Why aim for the top when the middle is so much closer?"

—Keith Sweitzer, 9, Dallas, Texas

CHAPTER 4

OCTOBER 15, 10:03 A.M. EVANSTON MIDDLE
SCHOOL. EVANSTON, VIRGINIA

"You want *me* to be a spy? With all due respect, I
don't think you want me. *I* don't even want me,"
Jonathan said honestly. "I'm not qualified to serve
our country. But I'd be happy to make sandwiches
for the people that do. My bologna and cheese is
acceptable."

"We don't need sandwiches. We need you," Hammett answered, and then turned to Shelley. "And you."

"Being a spy has been on my to-do list for a long

time," Shelley said, and then made a check mark in the air using her finger. "Shelley Brown, spy. I like the sound of that."

"I'm pretty sure spies don't use their real names," Jonathan pointed out as Hammett abruptly started pacing.

"It sure is a crazy thing to find you two right here in our own backyard, so to speak. You see, we've got agents all over this country looking for kids just like you. And trust me, you're not that easy to find, not these days, anyway."

"Just like *us*? Why would you want people just like *us*?" Jonathan asked.

"I'm the chief operating agent for the League of Unexceptional Children. What exactly is the League of Unexceptional Children? Well, I'm glad you asked."

Of course, they hadn't asked, but Hammett knew they would have eventually, and he didn't like to waste time.

"We are a covert network of spies comprised of this country's most average and utterly forgettable kids. Why average? Why not the brainiacs? Or the athletes? Or the beauty queens? Well, people remember those kids. They remember their names, their faces. They notice them when they walk into a room and they notice them when they walk out of a room. They are people with a footprint, a paper trail, an identity. But not you guys. You are the forgotten ones. You spend your days reintroducing yourself to kids you've known since preschool. And when people call on you, on the rare occasion it happens, they never call you by the right name. And you know why? Because you blend in. You are right there in the world's blind spot."

Jonathan and Shelley stared, mouths agape, at Hammett as he managed to praise them for the very asset that they each loathed—their averageness.

"President Eisenhower founded the League of Unexceptional Children after seeing how his granddaughter effortlessly eavesdropped while wandering around the White House. She was a nosy bugger, by all accounts. Really got into everything. And yet no one ever noticed her...she was too plain, too average, too unexceptional. Since that time, the League has reported directly to each successive US president. And while it is a poorly kept secret in the espionage world that the president has his own clandestine organization of spies, no one, not even the head of the CIA or the FBI, knows who they are or what they do."

"So you work for President Arons?" Jonathan asked in an attempt to keep up with the onslaught of information.

"Glad your ears are open, kid. It's an essential part of listening," Hammett said with a smirk before returning once again to his normal no-nonsense demeanor.

"I don't mean to interrupt, but I think there has

been something of a misunderstanding," Shelley said, raising her eyebrows at Hammett. "Because I'm actually pretty exceptional. I can break-dance. I speak Russian...*Lenin*...*Stalin*...*Borscht*..."

"Those are just names of dictators," Jonathan mumbled.

"And soup," Shelley huffed before returning her attention to Hammett. "I also regularly try new foods. Why, just last week I headed over to Koreatown—"

Jonathan shook his head. "Evanston doesn't have a Koreatown."

"No, but they have a Korean food truck, which is basically Koreatown on wheels. Now, as I was saying, I ordered a plate of kimchi. That's spicy pickled cabbage, for those of you who don't know. And get this, I loved it," Shelley stated proudly.

Hammett pulled the toothpick from his mouth. "We have pictures of you vomiting next to the food truck."

"Exactly. I loved it...until I threw up...and then—"

"Then you didn't love it so much," Jonathan chimed in with a self-satisfied grin that made Shelley's nostrils flare.

"I have a very strong gag reflex, so I vomit easily. Very, very easily. It just shoots out of me," Shelley explained.

"I don't want to talk about vomit," Jonathan said dismissively.

"Well, vomit doesn't want to talk about you, so burn.... You know what? That really didn't make any sense. I'm going to need to retract that comment." Shelley trailed off.

Jonathan furrowed his brow. "You want to retract your comeback?"

"You'll get used to it. I retract comments pretty regularly. I can't help it. My mouth talks, and three to five seconds later I realize what it said and sometimes it doesn't make a whole lot of sense."

"You can't retract comments. That's not how life works. People are responsible for what they say," Jonathan asserted.

Shelley threw up her hands and then turned to Hammett. "I think it's pretty obvious that I am nothing like this *unspecial* boy next to me."

"*Unspecial* isn't a word," Jonathan piped up.

"Well, it should be!" Shelley retorted.

"I hate to break it to you, doll," Hammett interjected, "but you're not special either. No one remembers you. Your talents leave you in the middle. And while you're strange, that doesn't change your unexceptional status. As a matter of fact, we have a lot of talentless weirdoes in our program."

Hammett then slipped his hands into his pockets and started tapping his left foot, his face awash with tension. "Now, as I mentioned earlier, we're in dire straits. Things are bad, real bad, which is why we had to move up your recruitment to the League of Unexceptional Children. You see, we've been following you two on and off for years, waiting until we thought you were ready, but due to an incident last night, we couldn't wait any longer."

"You've been following me? I feel like I should apologize. I'm a really boring subject," Jonathan said sheepishly.

"You are, kid, but it's one of the many reasons you are primed to save your country from the brink of disaster," Hammett responded.

"I've got to say, Hammy, Harold, whatever your name is—you really had me going there for a while.

This is a prank, isn't it? Come on, spill the beans! Who put you up to this?" Shelley prodded Hammett with a knowing grin.

"I'm going to be as blunt as an old razor. Neither one of you has any friends, or even foes, for that matter, so who would prank you—your pet goldfish?"

"How did you—" Shelley started before being interrupted by Hammett.

"That's right, doll, we know about your secret goldfish, Zelda. And frankly, we don't think her quality of life is very good in that closet of yours."

As Hammett spoke, Nurse Maidenkirk entered the sick bay carrying a clipboard under her right arm.

"I knew a woman named Zelda once. She's dead now," Nurse Maidenkirk stated as she removed a slip from her clipboard and passed it to Hammett. "Died from an infected paper cut. The first case in history."

Jonathan stared at Nurse Maidenkirk, wondering if the sour-faced woman had ever experienced a happy thought. Not that he was known for his optimistic approach to life, but even Jonathan found reason to smile from time to time.

"Someone could really use a puppy. Or a lep-

rechaun with a pot of gold. Or better yet, a lepre-
chaun with a pot of puppies," Shelley whispered to
Jonathan as Nurse Maidenkirk exited the room.

"That dame's a fine spy, one of the very best. Put
Maidenkirk in with a target for five minutes and
they'll spill their guts just to get her to stop talking,"
Hammett stated with genuine admiration. "But
don't let her give you any shots, you hear?"

Shelley and Jonathan nodded as it dawned on
them that Nurse Maidenkirk wasn't *actually* a
nurse. She was like an actress on television, just pretending. It was a frightening thought for many reasons, not the least of which was her propensity for
using students like pincushions.

"I need both of you down at headquarters after
school, but before I can give you the address, a few
facts need to be reviewed," Hammett said as he
unfolded the slip of paper from Nurse Maidenkirk.
"Neither of you speak a foreign language, correct?"

"No, but that will be dealt with shortly, as it's on
my to-do list," Shelley answered as Jonathan shook
his head.

"Have you ever received an A on a test after the
second grade? Anything prior to the second grade is

meaningless, since we all know they're only grading on a kid's ability to nap and maintain bladder control."

"No," Shelley and Jonathan replied.

"Have you ever been accepted onto a team? And remember, if a team doesn't reject someone, it isn't a real team."

"Definitely not," Jonathan answered, followed by Shelley's "No."

"Has anyone other than blood relatives ever attended your birthday party?"

"No," the two answered in unison.

"Have you ever taken part in a school play? It should be noted that an exception will be made if you played a tree, a rock, or any other background object without lines, as those are universally accepted to be pity parts."

"No," the two replied yet again.

"In that case I'll see you at four p.m. sharp," Hammett said as he pulled a silver case from his pocket, popped it open, and handed them a card.

"Famous Randy's Hot Dog Palace. Order a double dog with a side of mustard, two sides of relish, a can of diet Fanta, fourteen packets of ketchup, two straws, and seven napkins. Got that?"

"Uh...kind of," Jonathan mumbled as he scribbled the list on the back of the card.

"And, kids, keep your wits about you and your mouths shut. The future of this nation depends on it."

"My mom used to think Bs
were a disappointment, then
I started coming home with
Cs. That showed her!"

—Beatrice Valdes, 8,
Santa Cruz, California

CHAPTER 5

<079454-BV-LOUC-405>

OCTOBER 15, 3:28 P.M. THE METRO. WASH-INGTON, DC

Jonathan sat next to Shelley on the orange subway seats, still amazed by what he was doing—he was on his way to "headquarters" to become a spy.

"What do you think is going to happen today?" Jonathan wondered aloud.

"I think they're going to try and get to know us a little better, to find out things they might have missed while trailing us," Shelley hypothesized.

"Like what?"

"Like who are our personal heroes."

"Well, who is your personal hero?" Jonathan asked, pondering whether he even had one.

"Neil Armstrong, the first guy to go camping on the moon."

"Um, he was the first guy to *walk* on the moon, but he definitely didn't go camping," Jonathan stated with a burst of confidence; it was a rare occurrence when he got to feel like the "brains" in a situation.

"Of course he did! No one goes all the way to the moon and then just turns around," Shelley said, shaking her head.

"I'm getting a C in history, but even I know Neil Armstrong didn't sleep on the moon."

"What a wimp! He was too afraid to pitch a tent and sleep out there, wasn't he?" Shelley exclaimed.

"A wimp? He flew to the moon!" Jonathan countered.

"Why did I say that?" Shelley muttered with sudden regret. "I'm afraid to pitch a tent in my own backyard. Clearly, I'm going to need to make another retraction."

"Again?" Jonathan remarked before releasing a long sigh.

"Cut me a little slack, would you?" Shelley asked, throwing her hands in the air. "I've spent my whole life talking and no one has ever listened. Not even my own family. And when no one listens, mouths tend to go a little haywire, saying crazy things just to keep life interesting."

At this point, Jonathan's attention had shifted to making sure they didn't miss their station.

"See, you're not even listening!" Shelley huffed as Jonathan stood up.

"Come on, this is our stop."

OCTOBER 15, 3:46 P.M. FAMOUS RANDY'S HOT DOG PALACE. WASHINGTON, DC

The League of Unexceptional Children headquarters was hidden beneath Famous Randy's Hot Dog Palace in the heart of Washington, DC. Not that anyone could tell that from the outside. No, from the outside, Famous Randy's looked like a regular little fast-food joint with a counter and stools that ran along the walls, a couple of red booths for larger parties, and a condiments bar.

"Who should order?" Jonathan asked as he pulled out the card and went over the list of items.

"Talk about a no-brainer. Shells to the rescue," Shelley said as a large group of teenagers entered, lining up behind them.

"I didn't ask to be rescued, I was just trying to be polite," Jonathan said as Shelley walked up to the girl, no more than seventeen, behind the counter. Snapping her chewing gum and fiddling with her iPhone, she clearly wasn't interested in her job, let alone Shelley and Jonathan.

"We'd like to order," Shelley announced loudly.

"So order," the girl grunted.

"Okay, we are now going to order," Shelley said dramatically, as if to give the girl a heads-up that they weren't just any old customers.

"May I suggest you skip to the *actual* ordering," Jonathan advised as he handed Shelley the card with the list written on the back.

"We would like a double dog with a side of mustard, two sides of relish, a can of diet Fanta, fourteen packets of ketchup, two straws, and seven napkins."

The girl's entire demeanor instantly changed. She swallowed her gum, tucked away her phone, stood up straight, and made eye contact.

"Unfortunately, we're out of diet Fanta at the

moment. But we have some other choices if you'll follow me to the back."

And so Jonathan and Shelley walked behind the counter, past the cash registers, and into the kitchen.

"A double dog with a side of mustard, two sides of relish, a can of diet Fanta, fourteen packets of ketchup, two straws, and seven napkins!" the teenager yelled at the kitchen staff.

Hot dogs and buns were left to burn on the grill as the employees ran to an oversized refrigerator, flung open the doors, and removed the shelves containing pyramids of hot dogs.

"Hop in," the girl instructed.

"You're locking us in the fridge?" Jonathan asked with a horrified expression.

"Get in and push the back wall," the girl barked impatiently. "I've got a line growing out front."

"Okay," Jonathan said reluctantly as he crawled into the large fridge.

"Keep it together, Shells, and remember: Getting into a refrigerator is like riding a bike; it never gets easier, so you might as well just do it," Shelley whispered to herself as she climbed in, desperate for a burst of courage.

"Are we sure this is a good idea?" Jonathan asked Shelley as the teenage girl slammed the door behind them, leaving the two in complete darkness.

"Push the wall! Push the wall!" Shelley repeated anxiously.

"I'm pushing!" Jonathan yelped as he pressed his hands against the cold metal panel.

Within seconds, the back of the fridge opened, prompting both Jonathan and Shelley to sigh with relief.

"It's kind of like Narnia, only with a lot of pork products," Shelley remarked as she and Jonathan climbed out of the fridge and into a mundane office, complete with elevator music and an old secretary clacking away on a typewriter.

OCTOBER 15, 3:59 P.M. THE LEAGUE OF UNEXCEPTIONAL CHILDREN HEADQUARTERS. WASHINGTON, DC

The elderly secretary was humming to herself as she tapped away, seemingly unaware of their presence. However, just as Jonathan cleared his throat and prepared to say hello, she spoke.

"Have a seat, children. Mr. Humphries will be with you shortly."

And indeed, the woman was right. Seconds later, Hammett marched into the room like a man on a mission.

"Come on, kiddos, move your stompers, we've got work to do," Hammett said, and then pushed open a large wooden door, motioning for them to follow.

The sound of typewriters swishing, phones ringing, and people talking greeted Jonathan and Shelley as they entered the room. It was manic. Exciting. Headache-inducing. The League of Unexceptional Children headquarters looked more like a newspaper office from the 1940s than the center of a major modern espionage group. The main floor was filled with row upon row of telephone operators, all talking into headsets while simultaneously rapping away on large shiny black typewriters.

"I've never seen people work so hard, it's like they—"

"Don't have the Internet!" Jonathan interrupted Shelley.

"League—as we call ourselves for short, because who has time to say 'the League of Unexceptional Children' while solving issues of national security— uses old-school techniques to succeed in the digital age. Bottom line, no one can hack into your computer if you don't have one."

Hammett led Shelley and Jonathan into a wood-paneled room filled with approximately a hundred kids ranging in age from seven to eighteen. Within seconds every eye in the room was watching, examining, and inspecting Jonathan and Shelley. And though both had long fantasized about being the center of attention, the intensity of the moment left them more uncomfortable than satisfied.

Hammett raised his right arm and motioned to the crowd. "*This* is the League of Unexceptional Children."

Jonathan's eyes widened as he scanned the mass of normal nondescript faces, utterly amazed that they could be spies.

"I thought you said you didn't have time to say the full name?" Shelley questioned Hammett.

"Don't be a smart aleck—it's like a potato wearing a hat, it doesn't look good," Hammett snapped before throwing his toothpick into the garbage and continuing. "These are the best spies this country has to offer. Each and every one of them average, forgettable, and totally unexceptional. And yet they've all been deactivated. That's right, the whole League is on lockdown. Why? I'm glad you asked."

But of course, they hadn't asked.

"Because this guy," Hammett said as he pointed to the only other adult in the room, a robust man tucked away in the back corner, "also known as Arthur Pelton, opened the gate to the White House for an enemy. An enemy we are currently calling the

Seal, and please do not inquire about the name, as I'd rather not get into the story behind it—"

"I thought I was helping my country! I never meant to cause any problems! Why, if I ever find that good-for-nothing Seal, I'm going to break every bone in his body!" Arthur shrieked while wringing his hands.

"Listen up. At some point, we're going to need your help, so that means we have to keep you around. But it will be a whole heck of a lot easier if you don't start screaming every five minutes. Got it?" Hammett scolded Mr. Pelton, prompting the always-perspiring man to go back to eating his Famous Randy's hot dog.

"Time to move, kiddos," Hammett instructed Shelley and Jonathan as he led them out of the conference room and down a corridor filled with industrial gray filing cabinets and buzzing fluorescent lights that made Shelley feel as though she were entering the Twilight Zone.

Hammett's office was medium sized, with a large metal desk, two armchairs, and a small sofa. In the corner was a bar cart stacked high with sodas.

"Care for a pop? We've got just about every

brand name available. None of that generic stuff for you guys," Hammett said as he motioned toward the cart. "Just one of the many perks here at League."

Shelley turned and looked Hammett straight in the eye. "Soda is one of the main causes of obesity in America."

"Save it for health class, kid," Hammett grunted, and then grabbed a file from his desk.

"Or was it that obesity was one of the main reasons for health class in America?" Shelley wondered to herself.

"Take a seat, I've got a lot to go over," Hammett instructed as he sat down behind his large and imposing desk. "Last night the unknown entity we are referring to as the Seal broke into the White House. However, what makes this so unusual is that once on the grounds, he was able to bypass all security agents and cameras, which means that he knows the White House *very well*. So well, in fact, that he even knew where the president's secret vault was located, behind the medicine cabinet in the private bathroom off the Oval Office."

"What was in the vault?" Jonathan asked.

"The list of all active League operatives, as well

as the first of two codes necessary to access the White House's mainframe, which contains classified documents from the Department of Justice, the CIA, the FBI, and, of course, the president himself. And it's not that these groups or individuals are doing anything wrong, but of course that's not to say that they're doing anything right. To put it simply, every country has secrets: secrets that could jeopardize the safety of the citizens, secrets that our enemies could use against us, secrets that could ignite chaos in the streets."

Hammett suddenly paused, removed a new toothpick from his mouth, and shook his head. "But that's not all. The Seal also kidnapped the vice president of the United States, Carl Felinter. Not that anyone knows Felinter's missing; we're not even telling his own wife. It's too dangerous. Plus, it's a pretty easy cover; no one pays much attention to the guy. Then why would anyone kidnap him, you ask? Well, the president and the vice president are the only ones who know the second code. And you need both codes to unlock the mainframe."

"I really don't think I'm the right person for this job. I once tried to figure out where a drip in the roof was coming from, and I wound up flooding the attic," Jonathan confessed.

"Spoken like a true unexceptional," Hammett said with a smile before returning to his businesslike demeanor. "We estimate we've got a week before the VP caves and the Seal is able to access the documents and auction them off to the highest bidder."

Shelley gasped and then threw her hands in the air. "I think I just solved your problem, Hammett. Move the documents before the Seal is able to get the second code out of the VP."

"No can do. It would take over six months to create a backup system capable of housing this much information," Hammett explained.

"Drat," Shelley grunted as she pulled out a pen and a pad of paper and jotted something down.

"You're not even writing. I can see the paper. It's blank," Jonathan huffed loudly.

"That's because the mere act of pretending to write helps me remember things," Shelley said sheepishly.

"Only three people outside the president and vice president were aware of the vault—Secretary of State Harold Foster, the president's chief of staff, Alice Englander, and the technology expert who installed the safe, Gupta Nevers," Hammett informed Jonathan and Shelley as he started to pace.

"No need to worry, we're on this, we're going to figure out which one of them is behind the leak ASAP," Shelley declared, having returned to her usual self-assured manner.

"Oh, because you've done this before? Oh wait, that's right, you haven't! Come on, Shelley, haven't you heard of managing expectations?" Jonathan griped.

"Take it down a notch, there's no need to get your khakis in a bunch!"

Hammett snapped his fingers, refocusing Jonathan and Shelley's attention back to the matter at hand. "We need you two in the field no more than twenty-four hours from now. So we're going to train you as best we can with the time allotted. But, as the future of this country depends on the success of this mission, the president has asked MI5, the United Kingdom's top espionage group, to send two of their best operatives to help. Unfortunately, they can't get here for at least four days. And we can't wait four days."

"Are you sure you don't want to call the FBI or the CIA?" Jonathan asked in an uneasy tone, overwhelmed by the gravity of the mission before him.

"Those putzes! I wouldn't trust them to find a missing dog, never mind the vice president of the United States!"

"My English teacher told me that the only extraordinary thing about my essay was that I still didn't know how to spell *extraordinary*. Is it just me, or does it seem like there should be a hyphen in there?"

—Shamsi Houshmand, 11,
Vero Beach, Florida

CHAPTER 6

<088554-SH-LOUC-343>

OCTOBER 15, 5:02 P.M. THE LEAGUE OF
UNEXCEPTIONAL CHILDREN HEADQUAR-
TERS. WASHINGTON, DC

The room was cold. The air was stale with a faint
hint of both coffee and dust.

A threadbare American flag and the seal for the
League of Unexceptional Children decorated the
wall behind the brown lacquered podium. An olive-
green intercom, mounted next to the door, crackled
and buzzed.

"We have a 1982 Code Green. All agents are to

report to their positions immediately," an unknown voice boomed.

"A 1982 Code Green?" Jonathan repeated to Shelley as the two sat alone in the middle of ten rows of folding chairs.

"I bet the VP caved. And now the Seal is trying to sell his first document, maybe even the nuclear codes," Shelley hypothesized dramatically.

"The nuclear codes?! I hadn't thought of that… how on earth are *we*—two people who can't even manage to get Bs on spelling tests—being put in charge of this?" Jonathan asked with a hint of hysteria.

"Who cares? We're in charge and we're going to be awesome!" Shelley answered confidently.

"How crazy are you? Because only a crazy person would say that in response to what's happening. The codes that could blow up this whole country in a second might have just been sold to the highest bidder, and you're telling me that you actually feel prepared to handle the situation?" Jonathan exploded.

"Don't worry, I've got skills…skills to…buy some dills…" Shelley quietly trailed off.

"Dills? Are you talking about buying *dill pickles*?" Jonathan asked while shaking his head.

"I was, and I really couldn't tell you why. It just came out, which is weird since I don't even like pickles. I'm more of a sugar than a salt kind of girl," Shelley admitted.

"Has anyone ever diagnosed you with mental issues?"

"You mean like having a great personality? Because if so, the answer is yes," Shelley proclaimed. "And FYI, Congress is trying to pass a bill to ban khaki, so you may want to look into some other clothing options."

"Khaki is a great color," Jonathan responded as he looked down at his trousers. "It tells the world, 'I plan on paying my taxes when I grow up.'"

"*That's* what you want to tell the world? Boring...like, I'm already asleep."

"And what exactly does your outfit say?" Jonathan asked.

"Sociopath...or at least that's what I'm aiming for, anyway," Shelley answered.

"Great. I've been tasked to save my country

from destruction and my partner is a sociopath," Jonathan groaned.

"*Aspiring* sociopath," Shelley corrected Jonathan. "Apparently sociopaths are super successful."

Just then Nurse Maidenkirk and Hammett entered the room.

Shelley immediately jumped out of her seat and announced, "There's been a 1985 Code Green and Jonathan here thinks it's the nuclear codes, but not me. It's the president, isn't it? He's been kidnapped. I hate to admit it, but I had a feeling, one of my paranormal feelings, that this might happen."

"Quite the imagination, doll. A *1982* Code Green is the start of a Monopoly game in the lounge. We've got over a hundred grounded spies; we've got to keep them busy somehow," Hammett explained, his toothpick hanging from the left side of his lip.

"That was my second guess…Monopoly in the lounge," Shelley mumbled under her breath.

"I feel this is a good time to bring something rather serious to your attention," Jonathan interrupted. "Nurse Maidenkirk, Hammett—Shelley has admitted to me that she is a sociopath, which I think we can all agree is not the ideal for an agent."

Shelley turned and looked at Jonathan in disbelief before refocusing her attention on Nurse Maidenkirk and Hammett.

"I said I was an *aspiring* sociopath ... and believe me, I've got a great reason for wanting to be a sociopath: success. That doesn't really help my case, does it? That's probably what a sociopath would say. For the record, I haven't pulled the legs off a grasshopper or anything."

"I'm going to need a new partner," Jonathan declared firmly.

"One is born a sociopath, it is not something that can be achieved through sheer determination, Shelley," Nurse Maidenkirk clarified. "And Jonathan, the only way to get a new partner at League is for your old one to die."

"Have agents died in the line of duty?" Jonathan asked.

Hammett and Nurse Maidenkirk exchanged a tense look before averting their eyes.

"I'd take that as a yes," Shelley whispered to Jonathan. "A make-sure-you-have-life-insurance kind of yes."

"Come on, kiddos," Hammett said, "we need

to get you sworn in and off to training as soon as possible."

✳ ✳ ✳

Jonathan and Shelley stood before Hammett with their left hands in the air and their right hands on a book entitled *How to Make Great Popcorn in the Microwave*. Positioned off to the side, Nurse Maidenkirk acted as the event's official witness. Although she seemed far more interested in drawing horns on the man gracing the front page of the *Washington Chronicle* than the ceremony.

"Do you, Shelley Pauline Brown, promise to serve the League of Unexceptional Children with honor, dedication, and innate mediocrity? To be average amongst greatness? To be forgettable amongst celebrity? To risk your life for your country's liberties, all the while answering to the wrong name?" Hammett asked solemnly.

"I do," Shelley stated assuredly.

Hammett then turned to Jonathan and repeated the same speech.

"...to risk your life for your country's liberties, all the while answering to the wrong name?"

"I do, but only because you seem to really want me here, and because, well, what else do I have going on in my life? But let the record show, I have serious reservations about my capabilities."

"Duly noted," Hammett said. "By the authority vested in me by the president of the United States of America, I welcome you to the League of Unexceptional Children."

Jonathan and Shelley turned and looked at

each other. Hammett had been right. Ever since he uttered those first words, nothing had been the same. And as far as they could tell, nothing ever would be the same again.

"Unfortunately, kids, we don't have time to celebrate. We just received the vice president's confidential record and it's not good. It turns out he slept with a night-light until he was sixteen. He quit the Cub Scouts after burning his fingers making a s'more. And he has twice asked a doctor for local anesthesia to remove a splinter. This tells us he has a very low threshold for pain and suffering," Hammett stated in his usual rapid-fire manner, toothpick still hanging from the corner of his mouth.

"Ticktock, ticktock...time's running out," Nurse Maidenkirk interjected ominously.

Hammett nodded. "It's true, every second you kids aren't out there, this country is one step closer to obliteration."

"My math teacher told me
that if I believed in myself,
I could do better. It's not that
I don't believe in myself,
I just know myself."

—Hazel Nielson, 13,
West Jefferson, North Carolina

CHAPTER 7

`<080010-HN-LOUC-198>`

OCTOBER 15, 5:45 P.M. THE LEAGUE OF UNEXCEPTIONAL CHILDREN HEADQUARTERS. WASHINGTON, DC

Standing in the kitchen/break room at the League of Unexceptional Children, Nurse Maidenkirk squinted, lifted her left hand, and then thrust a metal dart straight at the front page of the *Washington Chronicle*.

"The press calls him the Cookie Monster because he's always eating cookies, whether walking into court or addressing the judge—there's a flurry of crumbs falling down his chin," Nurse Maiden-kirk said flatly before effortlessly tossing another dart directly at the man's left eye. "The name makes him sound warm and fuzzy. But that's not Alan Feith. He's a criminal who stole from the weakest members of society to get rich."

Nurse Maidenkirk then turned to Jonathan and Shelley, who were seated at the round table in the middle of the room. "When I was your age, I wanted to be a mortician so I could dress up dead people. But then I learned about criminals. And I hate criminals. That's why I'm here."

"Well, we're here for training…is that something you could help us out with?" Jonathan asked apprehensively.

"Hygiene is a very important part of espionage," Nurse Maidenkirk stated as she sat down at the table. "And I am not referring to *your* hygiene, although people have been known to lose limbs due to gangrene and other infections brought on by poor washing habits."

"I *love* antibacterial soap," Shelley bragged.

"As I said, I am not referring to *your* hygiene, but the hygiene of a scene. You may not be noticed when

76

you walk in. You may not be remembered after you leave. Your words may blend into the background. Your faces into the wallpaper. But your fingerprints do not disappear. Your DNA does not disappear, which is why you are to leave the scene exactly as you found it, without a trace of yourself. Do not blow your nose and leave the tissue in the wastebasket. It's a genetic calling card—"

"I never get sick, so that's not a problem for me," Shelley again interrupted.

"You know who I just heard was sick? Old lady Masterton. You know her, don't you? She's the one who lost a couple of fingers in a gardening accident last year," Nurse Maidenkirk said, looking down at Shelley's small, pale hands. "Speaking of fingers, you are to wear flesh-colored gloves at all times while on a mission," she continued while laying two pairs of latex gloves on the table, each matched to Jonathan's and Shelley's skin tones, complete with painted-on freckles and fingernails.

"We are so James Bond!" Shelley said excitedly as she tried on the gloves.

"You are not James Bond. You are James Bond's cousins who are routinely left out of the family newsletter for both a lack of interest and your relatives' general forgetfulness regarding your existence," Nurse Maidenkirk clarified. "Now, collect your things and go. Hammett is waiting for you on the Mall."

OCTOBER 15, 6:12 P.M. THE MALL. WASHINGTON, DC

The National Mall is technically a park, although it looks more like an outdoor promenade lined with gardens, the Washington Monument, the Lincoln Memorial, the Capitol building, and museums. And while it is a popular tourist destination, today it was being used as Hammett's training grounds for espionage.

"It's like Beijing. There are people everywhere," Shelley said to Jonathan as the two trailed Hammett along the Mall.

"So you've been to Beijing?" Jonathan asked skeptically.

"Beijing is a city in China where people eat really spicy food with chopsticks," Shelley said as though recalling a fond memory from long ago.

"But have *you* been to Beijing?" Jonathan pressed on.

"Ugh," Shelley groaned. "Why do you always have to listen to me?"

Seated on a park bench between Jonathan and Shelley, Hammett kept a copy of the *Washington Chronicle* folded in his lap. Shelley stared at the picture of Alan Feith, aka the Cookie Monster, pondering what he might look like if someone were to tame his large gray Afro. Having noticed Shelley's interest in the picture, Hammett promptly turned the paper over. "Alan Feith thought he was above the law. And let me tell you, kids, no one's above the law. You guys, however, are allowed to go *around* the law—but more on that later. First things first." Hammett took two nondescript blue pens from his jacket pocket. "Always carry these with you."

He then quickly pulled one of them apart, turning it into a strange pliers-type contraption.

"It's a lock breaker. It will get you into most homes and low-security businesses. Slip the straight bit in the top and the curly bit in the bottom and jimmy it around," Hammett said before returning the item to its regular form.

"But isn't it illegal to break and enter?" Jonathan wondered aloud.

"You've been tasked to save this country, and with that comes a little leniency," Hammett explained. "In other words, the president has given you the freedom to work *around* a few laws. Get it? Got it? Good."

"If only I'd been part of League when I was caught with black-market Girl Scout badges. Maybe I wouldn't have been dishonorably discharged."

"Black-market badges? You mean, you *bought* badges?" Jonathan asked.

"Listen, Judge Judy, you have no idea how hard it is to start a fire with a little bit of lint and a magnifying glass," Shelley replied defensively.

"Ticktock, ticktock," Hammett interjected.

"Sorry," Jonathan and Shelley mumbled in unison.

"In the highly unlikely event that someone recognizes you, they probably won't remember your name or how they know you. So redirect them. If they've got shiny white teeth and healthy gums, tell them you haven't seen them since you bumped into them at the dentist. If they look sporty, mention the gym. And if you can't get a read one way or another, mention the grocery store. Everyone goes to the grocery store. Well, everyone except for your parents, Jonathan—they go to 7-Eleven."

Jonathan nodded while Shelley looked on jealously—she loved 7-Eleven.

"Now, it's rare, but we have had instances where agents have been caught in—how should I say—compromising situations. Why, last year alone we had agents discovered illegally entering the Capitol building and the mint. Should this happen, there's only one thing to do: Show them your report card," Hammett said as he handed Shelley and Jonathan their very own pocket-sized editions of *How to Make Great Popcorn in the Microwave*.

"Inside this book, which you are to keep on you at all times, is a copy of your actual report cards, albeit with different last names. There are also pictures of Vice President Carl Felinter. We have found that a great many League operatives have no idea what our elected officials look like."

"Not me! I know Carl Felinter like the front of my hand...or is it the sole of my foot?" Shelley stopped to think. "Never mind, I know Carl. He's a short, bald man with an enormous stomach and an English accent."

"Doll, I believe you're describing Winston Churchill. And not only is he dead, but he was never vice president," Hammett corrected Shelley. "Also in the book are pictures of technology specialist Gupta Nevers; the president's chief of staff, Alice Englander; and Secretary of State Harold Foster— the only three people outside of the president and vice president who were aware of the secret vault."

"What's the point of the report card?" Jonathan asked as he flipped through the book.

"No one will think that a kid with straight Cs is working as a spy," Hammett replied.

"But what if someone sees us reading the book and is interested in it?" Jonathan speculated.

"No one will ever ask to look at a copy of *How to Make Great Popcorn in the Microwave* unless they're an agent too," Hammett assured the boy.

"I don't know about that. I've always wanted to know how to get all the kernels to pop without any of them burning," Jonathan expounded.

"That statement alone solidifies your place in the League," Hammett remarked, shaking his head.

The sky had morphed into a mix of pink and orange, highlighting the silhouettes of the skyline.

"Look at this place—gorgeous, isn't it? And just

think, somewhere out there the Seal's got our vice president—and heaven knows what he's doing to get that second code," Hammett said as he tucked the newspaper under his arm and stood up. "On your stompers, we need to move. Don't stay too long in one place. It attracts attention, and you never know who might be eavesdropping."

"I've been waiting my whole life for someone to eavesdrop on me," Shelley said wistfully.

Ignoring Shelley, Hammett casually peered around before speaking again. "Your job is to get information. Get in, talk to the target if necessary, and get out as fast as you can. By the time the target realizes your questions were a bit off the beaten path, you will be gone and all the target will have is a fuzzy memory of someone who doesn't exist. That's right, you don't exist because whomever they remember doesn't look a thing like you. Not one thing."

Jonathan stepped closer to Hammett and whispered, "And what kind of questions are we supposed to ask?"

"We will brief you beforehand. Now." Hammett smiled at them. "I think you're ready."

"Ready? You can't be serious!" Jonathan scoffed.

"Well, of course you're not *ready*, but the country is about to collapse. So unless you're *ready* to see this whole place crumble beside you, I suggest you find some courage," Hammett barked, wagging his index finger in Jonathan's face.

"Not to worry, I'm sure he has some courage hidden in there somewhere," Shelley jumped in. "For as I often say, behind every pair of khaki pants is a denim soul."

"That doesn't make sense, but thank you anyway," Jonathan muttered to Shelley.

Hammett pointed across the Mall. "We've got a man, approximately thirty-seven years old, in a red cable-knit sweater and gray slacks with a tan Pomeranian on a leash. I'd put the dog at five to six years of age, but with all that fur, it's a ballpark guess at best."

Jonathan and Shelley turned and scanned the promenade until they spotted the man with the Pomeranian.

"He's your training target. You are to approach with a story about being lost, looking for the Smithsonian, and ask if he can give you directions. While he is helping you, you are to find out his name and profession. But be careful; you mustn't attract suspicion. After getting said information, you are to leave. Get it? Got it? Good-bye."

"Wait! Before you go, can we discuss my character's background? Do I have an accent? Am I Latvian? Australian? Should I limp? To get the guy's sympathy, you know?" Shelley asked.

"You really are an eager beaver, aren't you? But listen, doll, you got this all wrong. This isn't drama class. Act like who you are, Shelley, only with a different last name. Understood?" And with that, Hammett headed toward a bench a few feet away, toothpick in mouth and hands in pockets.

"I guess we have to do this," Jonathan mumbled halfheartedly.

"The thing is, Johno—can I call you Johno?— I'm over all this training nonsense. We've been at it forever. And frankly, I'm itching to handle the bad guys," Shelley declared confidently.

"We've been training for a couple of hours. That's not even the length of a school day," Jonathan pointed out.

"In movies, training sequences are always cut together with really cool music. It's like boom, two to three minutes later, everyone's an expert."

"Good to know you keep your expectations realistic," Jonathan offered sarcastically.

"Johno, I think you should ask for directions, then I'll compliment his sweater, and after he says thank you, I'll ask the questions."

"That actually sounds reasonable," Jonathan admitted, surprised by Shelley's sudden burst of practical thinking.

The man in the red cable-knit sweater with the

tan-colored Pomeranian on a leash was now but a few feet away. Jonathan sighed and reminded himself that it was only a training mission; there was absolutely no need to be nervous. Walking next to him, Shelley exuded her usual mix of self-confidence and delusion, a combination Jonathan found reminiscent of his mother.

"Excuse me, sir?" Jonathan called out to the man. "Yes?"

"We're here visiting and we really want to see the Smithsonian, but we can't seem to find it," Jonathan muttered, smiling stiffly.

"Nice sweater," Shelley piped up, although the man didn't hear her, so she impulsively grabbed his arm. "I've always loved the color red. It's a shame it's the color of blood, especially since it rhymes with *dead*. Red dead. Dead red... You know what? I'm really sorry, but can I have a do-over? My brain just went haywire with excitement talking to you."

"Shelley! You can't ask the target for a do-over! That's super-unprofessional! Plus it makes you look insecure, and spies can't be insecure!"

"You're spies?" the man asked, barely stifling his laughter.

"Way to go, Johno! You told the target we're spies! Nice job!" Shelley scoffed, shaking her head with disappointment.

"Oh no, I did, didn't I?" Jonathan muttered quietly, his face crumpling with shame. "This is bad! Good spies don't tell people they're spies!"

"Maybe you're more of a mediocre spy?" Shelley suggested.

"What about you? Dead is red! The color of blood! Way to act normal!" Jonathan shot back.

"While I admit it wasn't my finest hour, I think we can both agree that I am the winner here because I didn't tell the man we're spies," Shelley stated triumphantly.

"There is more to being a spy than just *not* telling people you're a spy," Jonathan said, trying to convince himself as much as Shelley.

"But you've got to admit it's pretty important."

Jonathan suddenly looked around. They were alone. The man with the red cable-knit sweater and Pomeranian was nowhere to be seen.

"We lost the target," Jonathan uttered in dismay.

"That is definitely *not good* spymanship...wait, is *spymanship* a real word?" Shelley asked.

"You want a real word? How about *fail*? As in, you two just failed your training mission," Hammett snapped from behind Jonathan and Shelley. "Less than ten seconds and you two were barking at each other like a couple of rabid squirrels, completely losing sight of the target!"

"We're really sorry," Jonathan mumbled, his eyes trained on his shoes.

"We may have gone a little off course, but we'll do better next time, I promise," Shelley offered sincerely.

"There is no next time. Training is now officially over. So go home, lick your wounds, and sleep a full eight hours," Hammett instructed firmly. "Tomorrow morning you will receive a message in your locker with your first real mission."

"But we just failed our *training* mission," Jonathan said.

"That's right, so unless you plan on failing your country, I suggest you two straighten out your heads and get serious." Hammett bristled. "This is a war, and you're the only soldiers on the field... understand?"

"A man of moderate
intelligence once said that
it's okay to be average.*"

—Jude de Williams, 9,
Morgantown, West Virginia

*I made this up to make myself feel better.

CHAPTER 8

<095587-JW-LOUC-167>

OCTOBER 16, 7:03 A.M. EVANSTON, VIRGINIA

Seconds after the sun rose, Shelley jumped out of bed, fed her goldfish, Zelda (who was still hidden away in the closet), and tried on the first of several "spy" outfits. Shelley was aiming for cool, professional, and ready to take down the bad guys. Standing in front of the mirror, she practiced pulling out a badge, having forgotten that League operatives did not use badges.

"The name's Shelley Brown and you're going

down... darn it! I used my own name again! Zelda, I'm going to need a do-over," Shelley mumbled to her fish as she clenched her fists with frustration.

A few streets away Jonathan was standing in his bathroom, staring blankly at himself in the mirror. He wasn't up for the task. He was barely up for being alive, never mind rescuing the vice president of the United States and saving the country from possible invasions and rampant chaos. *Who knows*, Jonathan thought, *maybe anarchy wouldn't be that bad*. Maybe he'd kind of enjoy it, everyone doing whatever they wanted, when they wanted. *Wait a minute*, he thought, *that's the equivalent of letting my parents run the country—and that's a very, very, very scary idea*. Why, it was so scary, there weren't enough *very*s in the world to describe it!

Downstairs, Jonathan ran through the kitchen, grabbed his lunch from the fridge, and double-checked that he had both his pen and his popcorn book.

"What's the rush, champ?" Mickey called out as Jonathan bolted toward the front door.

"I'm off to save the world!" Jonathan replied as

he dashed from the house at 8:02 a.m., a full thirteen minutes before the neighborhood kids would hit the pavement.

"Looking for me?" A girl's voice jolted Jonathan as he exited the front door.

Standing next to his neighbor's elderly pug was Shelley, dressed in a green-and-brown tweed pantsuit.

Jonathan looked the girl up and down before asking, "What the heck are you wearing?"

"This, Mr. Khaki, is what I call Sherlock Holmes chic," Shelley answered, turning in a full circle to showcase her outfit.

"Sherlock Holmes was a detective, not a spy. And to be honest, you look more like someone who's about to jump on a horse and hunt rabbits," Jonathan confessed while eyeing the thick wool ensemble.

"I would *never* shoot a rabbit. Unless, of course, I was lost in a forest without any other options. Although I doubt I could skin it, and we all know I can't start a fire to save my life—"

"Or earn a badge," Jonathan added as Shelley

took off her Sherlock cap and hid it behind a shrub in front of his house. "What are you doing?"

"A little tweed goes a long way...."

"Come on, we've got to get to school and check our lockers. Hammett said there'd be a message regarding our first mission," Jonathan explained, pulling at Shelley's arm.

"Our first step in stopping the Seal and saving the country."

"And if we fail?" Jonathan asked.

"I don't know," Shelley answered. "Actually, I do. We'll have to move to a remote part of Canada in case it ever gets out that we're responsible for the greatest failure in history. Plus we'll probably feel super-guilty...like worse than the time I decapitated my sister's doll."

OCTOBER 16, 8:19 A.M. EVANSTON MIDDLE SCHOOL. EVANSTON, VIRGINIA

"Hey, Marcus! What's happening up there?" Shelley called out as she passed a six-foot-one basketball player on the way to Jonathan's locker. "You take care too! See you later!"

"Marcus didn't respond to you. He literally

did not look at you or say one word," Jonathan informed Shelley.

"That's not true. He sort of looked around as if to say, 'Hello, Shelley, wherever you are.'"

"I didn't see anything even remotely like what you're describing."

"That's because you're a Dougie Downer, a Negative Ned. You see the world through gray lenses. And I'm a Sunshine Sally, spreading joy wherever I go," Shelley declared, opening her arms as if to give some invisible person a hug.

Jonathan twirled the combination to his locker, his stomach in knots. He still didn't feel ready to be a spy. As a matter of fact, he didn't even feel ready to read a spy novel. And yet he was seconds away from receiving his first mission.

"You have a furry egg in your locker? That's super-weird. Like weirder than a kid who keeps all her baby teeth in a box under her bed," Shelley said, and then smacked her hand against her forehead. "Why did I say that? I have a box just like that. Although I also have a really good reason; I'm keeping them in case I ever need dentures."

"It's a kiwi. And clearly you didn't read *How*

to *Make Great Popcorn in the Microwave* last night. Because if you had, you would know that a kiwi means we need to head straight to Nurse Maidenkirk."

"Why not just leave a note? Or send us a text?" Shelley asked.

"Notes and text messages can be intercepted, but not a kiwi."

OCTOBER 16, 8:29 A.M. EVANSTON MIDDLE SCHOOL. EVANSTON, VIRGINIA

"An air-conditioning unit dropped two stories, knocking a man unconscious while walking in Old Town Alexandria this morning. Apparently, he can't remember a thing. Not that I'm surprised; the radio said his head looked like a chewed-up piece of roast beef," Nurse Maidenkirk shared immediately upon seeing Jonathan and Shelley in the infirmary.

"Good morning to you too," Jonathan grunted as Shelley shook her head at the odd greeting.

"If only I got interesting cases like that in here," Nurse Maidenkirk said as she looked around at the twelve empty beds in the sick bay.

"Do you want us to drop something on someone's head?" Shelley inquired as Nurse Maidenkirk narrowed her eyes at the young girl.

"Of course not. That would be a criminal act, and I loathe criminals."

Sensing they were getting off track, Jonathan jumped in. "I found a kiwi in my locker this morning."

"We are expecting your first assignment from President Arons in precisely two minutes and seven seconds," Nurse Maidenkirk informed Jonathan and Shelley as she switched on the mammoth television in the corner and pulled out a stenographer's machine and a collapsible stool from behind one of the beds.

A morning talk show, consisting of eight women crammed around a table drinking coffee and yelling at one another, was shortly thereafter interrupted by a blond and overly made-up news anchor.

"*We are now cutting live to the White House for a briefing from the president regarding the possible increase in ground troops*," the anchor stated before the screen jumped to President Max Arons standing at a podium with two American flags and a blue-and-white oval plaque of the White House behind him.

"Good morning, everyone," President Arons greeted the room of reporters, brushing his right hand against his left eyebrow. "Late last night I met with the Speaker of the House"—the president cleared his throat and scratched the left side of his head—"regarding his opposition to the deployment of further ground troops at this time."

Nurse Maidenkirk typed frantically, her fingers moving in an absolute flurry.

"However, he has assured me that should the threat increase, therefore endangering US Air Force bases in the region," the president said before twitch-

ing his nose a few times and scratching his right cheek, "he would reverse his current stance. Thank you very much. I will not be taking any questions at this time."

And with that, President Arons left the podium, and the channel returned to its regularly scheduled program.

"Interesting," Nurse Maidenkirk stated cryptically as she pulled the white paper from the stenography machine. "You're going to have company on this mission, and not the kind of company that you'll enjoy."

"I don't get it. He didn't even talk about anything that had to do with us," Jonathan said.

"Clearly, someone was listening with his ears instead of his eyes," Nurse Maidenkirk pronounced.

"No way! All that fidgeting was code?" Shelley said, and then clasped her hand over her mouth.

Jonathan lowered his eyes. His stomach sank. There was something about his fellow unexceptional "getting it" that made the boy feel even more lacking in intelligence than usual.

"Normally the president is able to convey messages by other means, but due to the high security at the White House following Vice President Felinter's kidnapping, which as Hammett mentioned is being kept top secret, the president is taking no chances."

Shelley rubbed her chin thoughtfully. "So what's the mission?"

"The president knows his chief of staff, Alice Englander, to be paranoid and, like a certain former president, Richard Nixon, she tapes all of her phone calls. We need those recordings to know what she's up to, which means you will retrieve them from the basement of her home...today."

"When you say 'retrieve,' do you mean we're going to break into her house and steal them?" Jonathan asked, wiping his sweaty palms against his khaki slacks.

"Yes, that is exactly what I mean. And as Alice Englander lives in Evanston, you two will need an adult companion; otherwise, you most certainly will be picked up for truancy."

"So you're coming with us?" Jonathan guessed.

"Absolutely not. I have to administer shots to the entire basketball team," Nurse Maidenkirk said while miming jabbing a needle into her arm.

"That means Hammy's in the house!" Shelley hollered excitedly.

"No. I'm afraid Hammett will not be accompanying you either."

"Then who's coming with us?" Jonathan asked.

"Someone who sweats a lot. Someone who yells a lot. Someone who eats a lot..."

"Like I always tell my little
brother, if you set the bar
low enough, anything can be
considered a success."

—Mel Brodovka, 14,
Pittsburgh, Pennsylvania

CHAPTER 9

<011098-MB-LOUC-239>

OCTOBER 16, 9:13 A.M. EVANSTON MIDDLE
SCHOOL. EVANSTON, VIRGINIA

"Someone who sweats a lot. Someone who yells a
lot. Someone who eats a lot," Shelley repeated back
to Nurse Maidenkirk. "I assume you're not talking
about my uncle Jerry. He's also a scientist like my
parents...just a really angry one with a perspiration
problem and an enormous appetite. I once saw him
eat an entire turkey by himself."

"Well, I once saw a woman choke on a turkey
bone," Nurse Maidenkirk added.

Shelley shook her head at the news and then asked, "Did she die?"

"No. I gave her the Heimlich maneuver. I even kept the bone she coughed up as a souvenir."

"Personally, I prefer a postcard, but that's just me...." Shelley trailed off as Jonathan snapped his fingers.

"You're talking about Arthur Pelton! The angry security guard from the White House, right?" Jonathan pressed Nurse Maidenkirk, clearly proud to have figured out the clues.

Nurse Maidenkirk nodded and then went on to explain that they were to meet Arthur Pelton at the bus bench next to Evanston's Metro station.

OCTOBER 16, 10:31 A.M. EVANSTON METRO STATION. EVANSTON, VIRGINIA

It had been a couple days since Arthur had been placed on leave from the White House, yet he was still wearing his uniform. And as usual, his hands and face were pink and puffy as a result of the suit being a size too small. Hunched over, eating a roast beef sandwich on rye bread, Arthur failed to notice the kids approach.

"Mr. Pelton?" Shelley said quietly as she took a seat next to him on the bench and opened up a newspaper.

"Shelley, we're supposed to be with Mr. Pelton, remember? There's no need to pretend you aren't talking to him," Jonathan pointed out.

"Rats! You're right, Johno." Shelley groaned. "Mr. Pelton, can we take it from the top? I'd like to redo my entrance."

"If only the White House would give *me* a redo, then I wouldn't be sitting on some bus bench instead of working, protecting this country from scum like that Seal! You know, I've never liked seals. Not one bit. They're just a bunch of big, fat, lazy beasts that spend their days barking for handouts. You know what I say? Get a job, you bums!"

"Just to be clear, you're talking about *actual* seals. Like the ones we see at the zoo?" Jonathan clarified.

"That's right," Arthur answered.

Jonathan sighed to himself. "This is going to be a long day."

"If you're on leave, why are you still wearing your uniform?" Shelley asked as she eyed the man's tight ensemble.

"I can't tell my wife that I'm on leave because I let some guy into the White House who took the vice president. She'd never understand. She'd say it was my fault."

"But it is your fault," Shelley weighed in as Jonathan stepped back, sensing the man's mounting anger.

"Let me tell you something, Miss Know-It-All. The Seal was like a snake charmer, using his voice to hypnotize me. So don't blame the vice president's kidnapping on me! Blame the Seal! Blame seals everywhere!" Arthur ranted nonsensically while Shelley lifted her eyebrows, as though to say "You can't be serious."

"You are absolutely right, Mr. Pelton. The responsibility for this situation belongs not only to the Seal but seals everywhere," Jonathan said with such conviction that he almost believed himself for a second.

"Thank you for understanding," Arthur said while shaking his head at Shelley. "Women. They don't get it."

"I've never been called a woman before, so thank

you," Shelley said while making a check mark in the air. "Another thing off my to-do list."

OCTOBER 16, 10:49 A.M. EVANSTON, VIRGINIA

According to Nurse Maidenkirk's instructions, Arthur was to stand guard outside Alice Englander's house while they broke in and retrieved the recordings. But upon arriving at the quaint white clapboard house with blue shutters and a red door, Arthur announced his own ideas. And, as usual, none of them were good.

"You two need me. I'm a grown-up," Arthur said while pointing at the deep wrinkles on his forehead.

"We actually don't need you *inside*, but we definitely need you *outside*," Shelley said as tactfully as possible. "And let me just tell you, outside is where the action is...not the breaking-and-entering action, but the watching action."

"Guys, I'm going to have to pull rank here. I'm coming in. I'm leading this mission," Arthur said, his pink hands resting on his hips.

"Pull rank? You're a security guard currently on leave for losing the vice president!" Shelley scoffed, and then turned to Jonathan. "And you call *me* crazy."

"Stop bringing up the vice president!" Arthur shouted, and then looked up at the sky. "This world sure isn't fair! You make one little mistake and you're done. Kaput! Gonzo!"

"Little mistake? I don't know if I would call it *little*—" Shelley said before being cut off by Jonathan.

"Look on the bright side, Mr. Pelton: At least you've left an imprint on this world. You're a part of history. You're the man who got the vice president kidnapped and may possibly even bring down the whole government," Jonathan offered with a smile.

"I hadn't thought of it that way," Arthur Pelton acquiesced, his eyes glazing over as he imagined his face in history books.

"Mr. Pelton, why don't you sit over there on that bench and think about the huge impact you've had on this country," Jonathan suggested.

"Okay, but if you see any potato chips in the house, grab them. My blood sugar is getting low," Arthur instructed Jonathan before waddling away.

"I never would have guessed, but you're really good at manipulating people. I'm kind of jealous," Shelley said, eyeing the boy with admiration.

"I'm not sure if that's truly a compliment, but as they say, beggars can't be choosers," Jonathan remarked as he scanned the street for any sign of snooping neighbors. "Come on, let's head around back."

Jonathan moved slowly, aware of each step. He was on private property. He was about to break the law for the first time. And not just some petty little law like jaywalking. No, Jonathan was about to break into the house of a woman he had never met. Regardless of the fact that the president of the United States himself had authorized the mission,

Jonathan still felt like a criminal. But what choice did he have? He had to do this for the greater good. And so he forced himself to continue putting one foot in front of the other.

Jonathan's reticence was in stark contrast to Shelley, who was almost skipping with delight. The moment had finally come. She was in the throes of something exciting. And for once it was *actually* happening, it wasn't some far-out fantasy that she escaped to when feeling down. It wasn't like the time she won *The X Factor* without even being a contestant. No, Shelley Brown was *literally* breaking into the president's chief of staff's home because she was a member of the League of Unexceptional Children.

"It's not illegal if the president asks you to do it," Jonathan whispered to himself as he approached Alice Englander's back door.

He then sighed, pulled out his special blue pen, and set about jimmying open the back lock. However, as the minutes passed, it became evident that Hammett's instructions had been insufficient.

"Move over, Johno, let old Shells give it a try."

"Go right ahead, *Shells*," Jonathan answered, relieved to let his fingers uncurl.

Minutes passed. The door remained locked. Jonathan was now sweating in places he didn't even know were biologically possible. Shelley's fingers were cramping as she pushed and prodded over and over again. Vice President Felinter's face popped into her head and soon she was imagining the man wailing in pain. And all because Shelley couldn't get the door open, she couldn't finish her mission.

"Maybe there's a doggy door we can use?" Shelley suggested while doing her best to hide her burgeoning panic.

"If Alice Englander had a dog, even a really dumb one, it would have started barking by now," Jonathan said, dabbing the sweat pooling along his upper lip.

"I can't stop thinking about Vice President Felinter being tortured!" Shelley cracked, grabbing hold of Jonathan's sweater. "We have to get in there! We have to save him!"

"I know," Jonathan answered, terrified by Shelley's sudden grasp of reality.

"We've been here way too long. We're lucky Community Patrol hasn't shown up yet," Shelley squealed as Jonathan ran his fingers through his hair.

"Should we call Hammett? Should we return to headquarters? Should we break a window?" Jonathan proposed frantically.

"Ticktock, ticktock..." Shelley whimpered.

"This isn't how spies are supposed to react when things go wrong, is it?" Jonathan asked.

"No, but at least we haven't told anyone we're spies today. That's an improvement from yesterday."

"Shelley, we're clearly not cut out to be spies. We're not smart enough. We're not brave enough. We're not *anything* enough. We have no choice but to tell Hammett the truth—we failed," Jonathan lamented as he grabbed the contraption hanging from the lock and yanked. But it didn't move. So he yanked again and again until finally the contraption fell out...and the door creaked open.

"We're in," Shelley said quietly as she turned her sweaty, ashen face toward Jonathan and smiled.

It was a small victory, an unexceptional victory, but a victory nonetheless.

Alice Englander's hallway was long and narrow,

covered in dark green wallpaper adorned with cherubs, which instantly reminded Shelley of a saying she never could keep straight.

"Johno, I know this isn't really the time, but by any chance do you know if the saying is 'Life's a bowl of *cherries*' or '*cherubs*'?"

"Cherries," Jonathan blurted out, his nerves still shot.

"I don't get it," Shelley muttered under her breath.

"Can this conversation wait until we've finished the mission?" Jonathan asked as he fidgeted with the skin-colored latex gloves covering both his hands.

Don't sweat on the carpet! Don't lose any hairs! Jonathan thought, terrified at the idea of leaving a genetic calling card behind while sleuthing around the house of a complete stranger.

"Of course," Shelley answered. "And may I say, Johno: As of a few seconds ago, you're doing a very good job on this mission. Like better than a bowl of cherries. And please don't feel any pressure to compliment me just because I complimented you," Shelley went on. "Because I really hate that...I only like genuine compliments...so again, please do not say anything about how great I'm doing unless you mean it...."

Jonathan said nothing.

"A lot of non-genius children of geniuses crave validation, but not me. I know I'm fabulous...I don't need anyone to tell me...I mean, sure, I've never been invited to the Genius Convention, but who cares? I've got better things to do with my time....Well, not always, but occasionally," Shelley rambled.

"You're doing a great job," Jonathan offered unconvincingly, prompting Shelley to smile as the two continued down the hall.

Thick beige carpet compressed beneath their feet as they passed the kitchen and formal dining room, both of which looked like they hadn't been used since the Bush administration.

"What about this door, Johno?"

"It could be a closet or another room or it could lead to the basement. There's only one way to find out. Open it."

And so Shelley did.

"Do you smell that?" Shelley asked as she started

down the stairs into what turned out to be the basement. "That's the scent of international intrigue."

"Or dampness," Jonathan added as he followed his partner into the small but impressively organized space; everything from the hot water heater to the window to the light switch to the laundry detergent was labeled.

Shelley suddenly pressed her latex-covered right hand against her forehead. "We left that seal-hating maniac outside on the bench. We'd better move quickly before Community Patrol finds him. Who knows what he might tell them?"

Jonathan scanned the basement before pulling out his cell phone, using the screen's light to read the plethora of labels: HIGH SCHOOL YEARBOOKS, TAX RETURNS, NAILS AND HINGES, and finally PHONE RECORDINGS.

"Hard to believe Alice Englander actually labeled the box PHONE RECORDINGS. Talk about making it easy," Jonathan said as he picked up a small brown box filled with flash drives.

"Poor Alice clearly never heard the saying 'Stay messy so no one can find anything worth stealing.' "

Jonathan shook his head. "No one's heard that saying because no one has ever said that except for you just now."

Once outside, Jonathan breathed a sigh of relief. Not only was the mission completed, but Arthur had managed to stay out of trouble. The rotund man was fast asleep, his head bobbing up and down as he snored.

"Can't we just leave him here?" Shelley asked as Jonathan started nudging the man.

"No. At this point I think we're as much his babysitter as he is ours."

OCTOBER 16, 3:04 P.M. EVANSTON, VIRGINIA

After handing over the box of Alice Englander's phone recordings at the League of Unexceptional Children headquarters, Jonathan and Shelley returned home to wait for further instructions. Seated side by side on Jonathan's couch drinking celebratory Coca-Colas, they emanated success.

Jonathan broke into a self-satisfied grin. "I know I shouldn't say this, but once we got inside the house, it was actually pretty easy."

"I know, right? After only one day, we've got this spy thing down. And do you know why? Because for once in our lives, we're naturals."

"You know, Shells, I think you might be onto something."

It was a happy moment. In fact, it was the happiest moment either Jonathan or Shelley had ever experienced. But it was to be short-lived.

"Hey! They're talking about the president," Shelley squealed as she pointed at the television. "Turn up the volume!"

A stern-looking anchor in a gray suit with a red tie addressed the public, carefully pronouncing every syllable as only newscasters do. *This morning's press conference regarding the increase of ground troops has everyone from comedians to fellow politicians speculating that President Arons has caught lice from one of his children, as he was seen scratching and twitching throughout....*

"Ha! If they only knew! Amateurs!" Shelley interjected.

"Right?" Jonathan seconded as the anchor switched to a clip of the vice president.

"And now on to Oslo, Norway, where Vice President Carl Felinter is currently meeting with King Harald and Prime Minister Solberg..."

"But that's impossible!" Shelley shouted at the television. "He was kidnapped! The Seal took him!"

Jonathan stared at the screen in disbelief, desperately racking his brain for a plausible explanation.

"Hello? Jonathan? Say something!"

"If the vice president is in Norway, then obviously he wasn't kidnapped."

"But Nurse Maidenkirk and Hammett told us he was!"

"The national news just played a video of Vice President Felinter. I think it's safe to say Hammett and Nurse Maidenkirk lied to us," Jonathan said as a knot the size of a football turned in his stomach.

"But what about President Arons's message for us?" Shelley pressed on.

"Maybe the news is right. Maybe the president has lice? Maybe it wasn't a message at all? Maybe Nurse Maidenkirk made the whole thing up?" Jonathan supposed.

"No, this can't be right," Shelley whimpered as

her glasses started to steam up, hot tears streaming down her cheeks.

"I think we need to at least consider the possibility that we've been had, that they—whoever they really are—tricked us into doing their dirty work. That there is no *League of Unexceptional Children*..."

TOP SECRET

"I consider myself neither
intelligent nor dumb,
but rather a fine mixture
of both."

—Cyra Shelton, 10,
Phoenix, Arizona

SECURE
DOCUMENTS

CHAPTER 10

<030094-CS-LOUC-537>

OCTOBER 16, 3:15 P.M. EVANSTON, VIRGINIA

"What are you talking about? Of course the League of Unexceptional Children is real! We went to its headquarters!" Shelley argued as she brushed away tears.

"We went to a space under a hot dog shop where Nurse Maidenkirk and Hammett told us the president of the United States is going to trust two nobodies to save this country from the brink of disaster. They said that there is a network of spies comprised entirely of average, forgettable kids like us. Think about that for a second; it's an insane idea! How could we have fallen for it? And worse, who are they? What kind of people would trick a couple of kids into stealing tapes from the president's chief of staff?" Jonathan screeched as he started frantically running his fingers through his hair. "Do they send kids to Guantánamo Bay?"

Shelley blew her nose loudly, wiped away a few rogue tears, and then sighed. "You're right. It doesn't make any sense. No one in their right mind would put two kids whose greatest claim to fame is being able to spell their own names correctly in charge of anything to do with mall security, let alone national security."

"We're Benedict Arnolds and we didn't even know it!" Jonathan remarked semihysterically.

"I don't know who Benedict Arnold is, which only further proves your point. Why would the president hire a know-nothing nobody to save the country?" Shelley said, and then dropped her head into her hands.

Jonathan placed the tips of his fingers on his friend's trembling shoulder.

"I don't want to be invisible for the rest of my life," Shelley uttered softly.

"I get it. It's not like I enjoy being a loser."

"You're not a loser, Johno. People remember losers."

"Sometimes when I wake up from a dream where I have friends, good grades, and a name people remember, I let myself stay in the fantasy for a bit...I imagine going to the movies with a group of kids, a teacher congratulating me on a job well done..."

"It's nice, isn't it?" Shelley said as she looked up at Jonathan and smiled weakly.

"Yeah, but it's not real. It's not who we are; we're nobodies. There's nothing special about us," Jonathan replied.

"We're nobodies, all right, but I wouldn't say there's *nothing* special about us. After all, we did just accidentally commit treason. We stole information from our own government."

Jonathan shook his head and sighed. "We broke so many laws. There's only one thing to do: Turn ourselves in."

Shelley shrugged. "Maybe we should bat around some other ideas? I'm thinking ones that don't involve juvenile detention centers or the authorities calling our parents."

"My parents would probably think it's cool."

Shelley pursed her lips and clenched her fists. "We can't let Hammett and Nurse Maidenkirk get away with this! We just can't! We need to stop them!"

"What do you suggest?" Jonathan asked.

"I don't know yet. But like the saying goes, when a door closes, check to see if the alarm's on and then break a window."

"That's not exactly right...but it gets the point across," Jonathan responded.

"We need to go straight to the top, we need to sneak into the White House," Shelley proclaimed, eyes wide with anticipation.

"Not to be a Negative Ned, as you've so kindly referred to me in the past, but I feel like breaking into the White House so that we can tell the president about breaking into Alice Englander's house is only going to get us more jail time."

"You may have a point there, Johno."

"Why don't we stay away from breaking any additional laws and try something traditional like making an appointment?" Jonathan suggested.

"I think getting a meeting with the president is kind of hard. I mean, he's the president of the United States of America, not the president of the local Dalmatian Appreciation Society...okay, that doesn't exist...but I wish it did...because I would totally join."

"Forget President Arons. We need a target who's approachable but has all the right contacts...."

"For instance?" Shelley asked, peering over the top of her glasses.

"The secretary to the secretary of Homeland Security."

"You mean the assistant?" Shelley clarified.

"We can't start at the top of the food chain; they'll never listen to us. Our best bet is to focus on someone less important, but with ties to someone very important."

"You know, beneath all that khaki, you've got some pretty good ideas," Shelley acknowledged as Jonathan located the number for the secretary to the secretary of Homeland Security on Google.

"You want me to call? I've been told I have a great phone voice. Although, technically, I'm the one who told myself that," Shelley babbled as Jonathan dialed.

"Is this the secretary to the secretary of Homeland Security? Well then, my name is...actually, I would rather not say what my name is, but I need an appointment with you this afternoon. It's regarding a group impersonating government spies....How old am I? I think we're veering a bit off topic here, don't you?" Jonathan said as Shelley grabbed the phone.

"Hello? Shells here. Listen, we need to sit down with you ASAP. And yes, I know we sound crazy, but we're telling the truth. It just so happens that sometimes the truth sounds like a lie."

Click.

"Hello? Hello?"

"I take it she hung up," Jonathan surmised.

"How are we going to get anyone to listen to us?" Shelley grumbled as she grabbed a newspaper off the coffee table and started flipping through it. "Where are the classifieds? We need to hire a lawyer! People listen to lawyers!"

"That's the comics section. My parents throw the rest away," Jonathan explained before suddenly jumping to his feet. "We've been going about this all wrong. We can't go straight to the politicians. We need to go to the people the politicians listen to!"

"You mean their mothers?" Shelley asked.

"No, I mean the press," Jonathan answered.

"Does this mean we get to be on television? Because that's also on my to-do list."

"Shells, we're not going to a television station, we're going to the *Washington Chronicle*."

OCTOBER 16, 6:03 P.M. THE <u>WASHINGTON CHRONICLE</u>. WASHINGTON, DC

The *Washington Chronicle* was one of the country's most prestigious papers, not that anyone could tell from its nondescript white facade that looked as much like the headquarters for an insurance company as it did a newspaper. And yet it was inside these walls that some of the most important moments in history made their way to the public. Scandals. Triumphs. Tragedy. The *Washington Chronicle* had covered it all.

"So, have you ever read the paper?" Jonathan

asked Shelley as the two stood outside *Chronicle* headquarters, in front of the lobby doors.

"Is that your way of asking if I can read? Because I can," Shelley stated emphatically. "Although I will admit I'm not a very good speller, and that if it weren't for spellcheck, I probably wouldn't have passed the third grade."

"No, I meant do you follow any specific journalists?"

"Do you?" Shelley countered.

"No," Jonathan admitted quietly. "There's just

so much to look at online, I never make it to the *Chronicle*."

"So we've never read the paper. Big deal. We're twelve. We just need to go in there and ask for the youngest, hungriest reporter and then tell the truth," Shelley proclaimed confidently.

"Shells, you're right. We don't need a star reporter, we just need someone who will listen."

From behind Jonathan and Shelley came a woman's voice. "Excuse me, kids, but would you happen to know the way to the Smithsonian?"

"Sort of," Shelley said as she started to turn around.

Only before either Jonathan or Shelley could see who was talking to them, everything went black.

"For the last time, Mom, my
name is Jerry, not Fred!"

—Jerry Franklin, 11,
Spearfish, South Dakota

CHAPTER 11

<055749-JF-LOUC-874>

OCTOBER 16, 8:19 P.M. UNKNOWN WARE-HOUSE. WASHINGTON, DC

Jonathan and Shelley were seated. This much they knew. They also knew that their hands were tied tightly behind their backs and that thick burlap sacks covered their heads. But they hadn't a clue where they were or who had taken them, although they each had their ideas.

"Maidenkirk, I expected more from a pretend nurse than this!" Shelley screamed through the sack.

"I know what you guys are thinking, but honestly, we were just hanging out in front of the *Washington Chronicle* like normal twelve-year-olds do. It had absolutely nothing to do with you guys," Jonathan rambled nervously.

"I think what Jonathan meant to say is that we were down there for a school project about newspapers," Shelley clarified.

In a flash the burlap sacks were lifted and Jonathan and Shelley found themselves staring straight into the bright light of two large fluorescent lamps.

"Is this really necessary?" Jonathan groaned.

"Nurse Maidenkirk? Hammett?" Shelley called out as she tried to see the faces of the two captors standing over them.

"I'm not Maidenkirk. I'm Natasha," a woman said with a thick, unidentifiable accent.

Shelley offered a tight and phony smile. "It's nice to meet you, Natasha. Well, maybe not *nice*, but I'm trying to be polite since you're my kidnapper and all...."

"So you vork for Hammett?" a man's voice boomed.

"Work? No. Absolutely not. We were manipulated by Hammett, which is totally different," Jonathan corrected the man.

"They vork for Hammett, Igor. Don't listen to their lies," Natasha hissed.

"Seriously, we don't even like Hammett. We're never talking to him again! We're not even going to send him a Christmas card or a Hanukkah card or even just a happy New Year's card!" Shelley prattled on.

"You guys don't want *us*. We're just a couple of nobodies who got tricked," Jonathan chimed in, trying his best to keep his voice calm and casual.

"You know, Jonathan, your mom and dad are a lot of fun. They aren't your typical parents. Igor and I vere very impressed."

"How do you know my parents?" Jonathan asked.

"Oh, I guess you haven't noticed yet? Your parents are vith us. And that's vhere they're going to stay until you do vhat ve tell you," Natasha growled.

"You kidnapped his parents? Nobody kidnaps *parents*! Kids? Pets? Sure! But parents? Never!"

Shelley yelled, all the while squinting from the over-whelming brightness of the lights.

"Shelley, how different your personality is from your mom's and dad's—it's quite surprising," Igor stated calmly.

"What have you done to my parents? They're geniuses. The world needs them!"

"Mine aren't geniuses, but I need them!" Jonathan yelped.

"You vill take a message to Hammett tonight," Igor commanded. "Once ve have received vord that the task has been completed, ve vill let your parents go."

"We'll do whatever you want, just don't hurt them," Shelley pleaded.

"You're to tell Hammett that 'Victoria and Albert take marmalade on their toast,'" Natasha ordered as she leaned closer to Jonathan and Shelley, her face still obscured by the bright light.

"'Victoria and Albert take marmalade on their toast'?" Shelley repeated. "What does that mean?"

"It's a code, you moron!" Natasha bellowed, and then dropped the burlap sacks over Jonathan's and Shelley's heads, once again plunging them into total darkness.

The sound of tires screeching and brakes squealing alerted Jonathan and Shelley that something was about to happen. The van abruptly stopped. The door slid open. Their hands were untied. A swift kick to their bottoms sent them flying out the back of the vehicle onto the sidewalk. And by the time either was able to remove the sacks from their heads, their kidnappers were long gone.

Seated on the curb, Jonathan and Shelley looked around; there wasn't a person in sight, leaving them without a witness to confirm that two twelve-year-olds were tossed from a van with bags over their heads.

"I don't want to scare you, Shells. But we're involved with some bad people. The kind that wouldn't think twice about hurting our parents or us," Jonathan said, his voice shaky and uncertain.

"I've always felt like an outsider in my family. For a while I even thought I had been adopted as part of some experiment about the effects smart parents have on dumb kids. But after doing a mail-away DNA test, I found out that wasn't true."

"Shells? What are you talking about?"

"I know my parents have never shown much interest in me, but they love me. And I don't want anyone to hurt them," Shelley answered honestly.

"So what do we do? Should we go to the police?"

"It's too risky. Plus, we have no proof that any of this even happened," Shelley replied.

"So I guess that means we're heading back to Famous Randy's Hot Dog Palace," Jonathan mumbled.

Shelley nodded. "If only we knew karate…"

"Forget karate. If only we were real spies, then we might actually stand a chance."

OCTOBER 16, 11:06 P.M. FAMOUS RANDY'S HOT DOG PALACE. WASHINGTON, DC

Famous Randy's was a beacon of light in the night, literally glowing from the array of neon signs in its window. Deserted except for a teenage boy working behind the register, Jonathan and Shelley watched the place from across the street.

"I wish there were a few customers, or should I say witnesses," Shelley muttered, pushing her smudged glasses closer to her eyes.

"The place looks so scary. Did it always look this scary?" Jonathan wondered.

"No, but then again, we thought they were saving us from a life of being called Sally and Jeff."

"There's no point standing out here all night. It's not going to get easier. We just have to do it. We have to walk in there, give Hammett the message, and then calmly tell him that we would prefer he never contact us again."

"Johno, that is crazy polite. And since I highly doubt we'll ever make it out of there, I say we go big. Tell him that if he ever comes near us again, we'll mess up his slick hair! Rip apart his fancy suits! Stab him with a million toothpicks!"

"I don't want this to sound rude, but I would appreciate it if you didn't talk while we were in there," Jonathan stated candidly.

"Fine, but can I at least give them dirty looks?" Shelley asked.

"Sure."

"Okay, you've got a deal," Shelley said, offering her hand to shake.

After ordering a double dog with a side of mustard, two sides of relish, a can of diet Fanta, fourteen packets of ketchup, two straws, and seven napkins, Shelley and Jonathan once again found themselves in an oversized refrigerator surrounded by hot dogs. However, the second the door closed, both Jonathan and Shelley realized what they had done—they had willingly walked into their own personal jail cell.

"This was a trick, wasn't it? We're going to die in here! We're going to die smelling like hot dogs! And I don't even like hot dogs!" Shelley screamed, her voice reverberating off the metal walls.

"Stop yelling!" Jonathan said as he pushed against the back of the fridge.

"We're dead! We're as dead as the pigs in these hot dogs!"

"Ugh," Jonathan grunted as he pushed with all his might against the metal panel.

"It's not opening!" Shelley cried.

"I know it's not opening! I'm the one who's pushing it!" Jonathan snapped as a flood of hot dogs streamed past his head.

"What are you doing?" Jonathan griped.

"I'm trying to help!"

"By throwing hot dogs at me?"

"Yes!" Shelley cried loudly.

"Would you stop screaming? Your voice is frightening the few muscles I have in my arms!" Jonathan shrieked, and then rammed his shoulder firmly against the back of the fridge.

A crack of light cut through the dark space.

"We're getting out! We're going to live!" Shelley blubbered.

"At least for another few minutes," Jonathan muttered as he climbed into the office.

OCTOBER 16, 11:13 P.M. THE LEAGUE OF UNEXCEPTIONAL CHILDREN HEADQUARTERS. WASHINGTON, DC

"May I help you?" the elderly secretary asked without even looking up from her typewriter.

"Jonathan and Shelley here to see Hammett Humphries, or whatever his name really is," Shelley replied as she picked small bits of hot dog off her shirt.

"Have a seat," the secretary answered before whispering into the intercom.

Minutes passed. Jonathan and Shelley waited.

They tapped their feet. They cracked their fingers. They heard something rattle. They looked up. The air vent was shaking. Two screws fell to the floor, followed by the metal grate.

"At least we're going to have exciting deaths," Shelley muttered to Jonathan as a tall, lithe girl with shiny black locks and light brown skin climbed out of the air duct and dropped to the floor.

"Jonathan? Shelley? Follow me," the girl said in a refined British accent.

"Who are you?" Jonathan asked as he and Shelley slowly stood up.

"I only answer questions posed by my superiors," the girl replied coolly as she opened the large wooden door into headquarters.

Row upon row of operators typed and talked, seemingly unaware that it was fast approaching midnight.

"You think they're here of their own free will?" Jonathan whispered.

"No way," Shelley answered. "You can lead a horse to water, but if you want it to drink, you have to threaten it, or feed it something salty."

"That makes absolutely no sense."

"Well, maybe that's because you haven't spent much time around horses," Shelley said as the girl stopped and grabbed hold of a shiny brass doorknob.

"Hammett and Nurse Maidenkirk have been waiting for you," the girl announced as she motioned for Jonathan and Shelley to enter.

Seated at a rectangular table in a wood-paneled conference room were Hammett, Nurse Maidenkirk, and a blond-haired boy, approximately fourteen years of age.

"Thank you, Vera," Hammett said to the girl, and then turned to Jonathan and Shelley. "Hey, kiddos, we've been looking for you."

"Oh . . . have . . . you?" Jonathan stammered, his voice cracking under the stress.

"We went by your houses, by school, even to a few hospitals, but there was no sign of either of you, which was strange, seeing as I told both of you to wait at home for further instructions," Hammett recalled in his usual rapid-fire manner, albeit with a thick air of suspicion.

"Operatives sometimes find themselves injured, permanently so, after running away," Nurse Maidenkirk added creepily.

"When an operative willingly disappears, it's not called running away, it's called going AWOL," Hammett corrected Nurse Maidenkirk, and then popped a toothpick into his mouth.

"We would prefer—" Jonathan began as though reading from a teleprompter.

"Listen, Hammett," Shelley jumped in, prompting Jonathan to shudder, terrified of what she might say. "We're not interested in being used as pawns in your little game anymore."

"This isn't a chess match, doll. This is the future of the free world!" Hammett barked as he banged his left fist on the table.

"This is why I asked you not to talk," Jonathan hissed at Shelley, and then turned to Hammett and Nurse Maidenkirk. "We don't want any trouble, we just came here to give you a message."

"You mean that Victoria and Albert take marmalade on their toast?" Hammett offered with a sly smile.

"What? How do you know that?" Jonathan exclaimed.

Hammett motioned toward the girl and boy.

"Jonathan and Shelley, meet Vera and Felix from MI5, or to be more precise, MI5's covert ops division, made up of overachieving, tech-savvy teenagers. We weren't expecting them for a couple more days, but lucky for us, they were able to get here earlier than planned."

"We've already met," Vera remarked smugly.

"Of course you have, I almost forgot," Hammett said, nodding. "Good old Natasha and Igor."

"Velcome," Vera and Felix offered simultaneously.

"You're Natasha? You called me a moron!" Shelley growled.

"Look, we just want you to let our parents go and leave us alone! That's it!" Jonathan hollered, frustrated by his inability to keep up with all that was happening around him.

"Cool your jets, kid," Hammett responded. "Your parents are at a carnival in Arlington. And the Browns are safe and sound in Germany. We never touched them. We just needed to get you back in here before you were able to let too many cats out of the bag, if you know what I mean."

Nurse Maidenkirk carefully adjusted her small white nurse's cap and then looked straight at Jonathan and Shelley. "I can't tell you how surprised we were to discover you at the *Washington Chronicle*. Newspapers aren't the kind of places we expect to find our operatives."

"You lied to us. The vice president wasn't kidnapped. He's in Norway!" Jonathan screeched. "You tricked us into committing treason! We broke into Alice Englander's house and stole confidential recordings!"

"Oh, this must be about the video," Felix suddenly piped up. "That was my idea. I thought it smart to release something preemptively before the press had a chance to wonder about the vice president's whereabouts. We overlaid film from his trip to Vietnam with stock footage from Norway. And if I may say so myself, the finished product is near flawless."

"You're lying. The news said he met with the king and prime minister!" Jonathan snapped.

"No need to lose your cool; there's a very simple explanation for that. Vera and I asked the Norwegian government to go along with the story, which was hardly a problem, as we have such *spectacular* contacts in Scandinavia," Felix added haughtily.

"By the way, Scandinavia refers to Norway, Finland, Denmark, Iceland, and Sweden. And if you're confused, I'd be more than happy to point out the countries on a map for you," Vera added condescendingly.

"FYI, we love Scandinavia. We know everything about it," Shelley lied, pulling off her glasses to glare at Vera.

"I definitely wouldn't say we know *everything* about Scandinavia," Jonathan mumbled.

"Kiddos, I'm sorry we weren't able to warn you about the fake footage before it aired. But here's the thing: Nothing has changed. The vice president is still missing and we're still facing the release of classified documents. And should that happen, life as you know it is over. Bottom line: There's no time to waste; we need to get you back in the field."

"What about *them*?" Shelley asked, her nose turned up to demonstrate her deep dislike of Vera and Felix.

"You've got a little extra help in the form of these two. Consider yourselves lucky," Hammett said while nodding toward Felix and Vera. "And we can cross Alice Englander off the list. We've listened to her recordings. She's incapable of planning a birthday party, never mind a kidnapping and the possible destruction of the US government."

Jonathan shook his head. "How do we know you're telling the truth?"

"Yeah! You guys could be lying about the fake video of the vice president!" Shelley pounced.

"Open your peepers, kids. This here is the real

thing. You think anyone in their right mind would go to this much trouble just to get you to break into one lousy house? Come on! If you think that, then you've cracked up!" Hammett huffed. "Now give it to me straight: Are you in or are you out?"

"You can do anything you
put your mind to.*"

—Mr. Saul Greenberg, 56,
Brooklyn, New York

*This isn't true, but the school board still
makes me say it.

CHAPTER 12

<009802-SG-LOUC-054>

OCTOBER 16, 11:59 P.M. THE LEAGUE OF UNEXCEPTIONAL CHILDREN HEADQUAR-TERS. WASHINGTON, DC

"We're going to need a minute to discuss things," Shelley informed Hammett and Nurse Maidenkirk, both of whom nodded in response.

Shelley then grabbed Jonathan's arm and whipped him around, offering their backs to the room.

Jonathan leaned in, mere inches from Shelley's face, and whispered, "What do you think?"

"Vera is *seriously* annoying."

"No," Jonathan groaned through clenched teeth. "Do you believe Hammett? Can we trust him?"

"I always go with my gut."

"Okay, but what does your gut say?" Jonathan pressed.

"What does your gut say?" Shelley countered.

Jonathan yawned and then rubbed his eyes. "My gut is exhausted. It's so late, I can barely see straight, but if I had to guess, I'd say Hammett is telling the truth."

"I'm leaning that way too," Shelley said, before adding, "Now can we talk about how annoying Vera is?"

"No," Jonathan answered.

"Fine," Shelley relented. "Then can I at least tell Hammett our decision?"

"Be my guest," Jonathan replied as the two turned to face the room.

"Hammett, Jonathan and I have given a great deal of thought to the situation, because, as you know, we are *thoughtful* individuals—"

"No need for all this chitchat. A simple yes or no will do," Hammett interrupted.

"Where's the fun in that?" Shelley mumbled to herself, and then answered, "Yes."

"Welcome back, kiddos."

Jonathan sighed as he looked over at Shelley, whose eyes were starting to flutter as she fought off fatigue.

"Shells," Jonathan whispered as he tapped the girl's arm.

"What time is it?" Shelley asked groggily, looking at her watch. "It's after midnight! I need to get home before my grandparents call the police!"

"I wish I could say the same, but my parents don't believe in curfews," Jonathan grumbled.

"I wouldn't worry, doll. Your grandparents are having a card game tonight and they asked you to stay in your room, remember?" Hammett reminded Shelley.

"How do you know that? Did you hack my grandma's e-mail account?"

"We're spies, kid. We know everything. Well, not everything. We don't know where the vice president is, which is why as of tomorrow morning we're putting Felix and Vera on the tail of IT specialist Gupta Nevers. And you guys are going to follow Secretary of State Harold Foster," Hammett announced.

"With all due respect, don't you think we should follow the secretary of state, considering our vast and notable experience in the field?" Vera questioned Hammett.

"It's true. Vera and I have successfully shadowed prime ministers, dictators, Scotland Yard agents, and royalty. We are professional spies. We have been trained by the best. We have special equipment. To be frank, it's rather shocking that you're even considering putting such skill to waste by having us follow some IT guy," Felix huffed.

"No need to grandstand, kid, I've seen your résumé," Hammett said, a toothpick hanging from the right corner of his mouth. "But here's the thing: The president believes Gupta Nevers is the more likely suspect, so he's asked that you two tail him."

"So now that they're here, we're second-tier spies?" Shelley scoffed.

"I'm fine with the second tier. Honestly, after today I might even prefer it," Jonathan muttered.

"It isn't personal, Sarah," Vera interjected. "It's espionage."

"Her name's Shelley, not Sarah," Jonathan barked.

"Thanks, Johno," Shelley whispered, all the while scowling fiercely at her nemesis across the room.

"My most sincere apologies, *Shelley*," Vera offered unconvincingly.

"Fine, you can have Gupta Nevers, but not because you're better spies!" Shelley raged, wagging her finger in the air.

"Although you are," Jonathan added quietly.

"We'll take the easy target this time, but only because my partner is worried that stress is causing his hair to fall out!" Shelley declared dramatically.

"I've never even mentioned my hair," Jonathan corrected his friend.

"Sorry to hear about the male pattern baldness, lad. Tough break," Felix called out to Jonathan from across the room.

"Knock off the gabbing and go home, kids. We need you back here at seven a.m. sharp," Hammett instructed his operatives.

"So we're missing another day of school?" Jonathan asked.

"Tomorrow is Saturday," Felix stated, stifling a laugh.

"He knew that!" Shelley blurted. "Or at least I think he knew that...I can't say for sure since I didn't know him when he learned the days of the week."

"Please stop. Your *help* is making this so much worse," Jonathan whispered to Shelley.

"I can't say that's the first time I've heard that."

OCTOBER 17, 6:42 A.M. THE METRO. WASHINGTON, DC

Jonathan and Shelley sat bleary-eyed on the Metro, both absolutely exhausted from the previous day's events. They had managed to get five and a half hours of sleep, which was about half of what they needed.

"I know we were only kidnapped for a few hours yesterday, but I have to tell you, it was super draining. I've never been so tired in my life," Shelley grumbled to Jonathan, wiping the sleep out of her eyes.

"Yesterday feels like a dream. A really long dream with some annoying British people at the end."

"Ugh, that Vera thinks she's so sophisticated," Shelley complained, her fists tightly clenched.

"Is Vera, by any chance, the reason you're wearing this outfit?" Jonathan asked, eyeing Shelley's choice of a yellow skirt suit paired with a frilly blouse and an oversized pearl necklace.

"Do you like it? It used to belong to my great-aunt Ginny. I found it in the attic. I think it says young yet chic."

"I'm not really getting *young* from this look...."

"Then what are you getting?" Shelley questioned Jonathan.

"More of a senior bingo night at the YMCA."

"I can work with that."

"One of the great perks of being able to speak twelve languages fluently is that I'm a real whiz with vocabulary. I can nearly always deduce a definition once I've isolated the root of the word," Felix bragged to Jonathan from across the conference table.

"I guess you're really good at Scrabble, then," Jonathan replied flatly.

"Scrabble? How quaint. I haven't had more than an hour's downtime in three years. Not that I mind. I take my job very seriously, as I'm sure you do."

Shelley suddenly banged her fist on the table, garnering everyone's attention. "Jonathan's the most dedicated operative I know. As a matter of fact, he even wants to get a League of Unexceptional Children tattoo when he turns eighteen."

"Actually, I'm not really a tattoo kind of guy," Jonathan added.

"I don't think it would be very intelligent to advertise a secret organization in the form of a tattoo," Vera chimed in, brimming with smugness.

"That's why Jonathan was planning to do it on the roof of his mouth. That way only his dentist would know…and he has a very trustworthy dentist…." Shelley poorly covered.

"Again, I have no such plans," Jonathan uttered quietly.

Following the end of the tattoo conversation, Jonathan, Shelley, Felix, and Vera sat in silence, each hoping that Hammett or Nurse Maidenkirk would walk in and end the rampant awkwardness.

"What are your thoughts on the latest spy fly?" Felix finally broke the silence. "We just tested model 4B, and we were quite impressed."

"We also tested model 4B and we were *not* impressed," Shelley bluffed.

Jonathan shook his head. "We've never even heard the term *spy fly* before."

"You've never heard of a spy fly?" Vera remarked disbelievingly. "It's a flying audio and video recorder the size of a pea that moves with the precision of an insect, making it nearly undetectable."

"And that's legal?" Jonathan asked.

"As you'll soon learn, *legal* is a relative term in the espionage world," Felix answered.

"From the looks of it, they both have quite a bit to learn," Vera commented under her breath.

Shelley took off her glasses and cleaned them carefully on her shirt. And not because they were dirty, but rather to keep her hands occupied so that she didn't *accidentally* strangle Vera. Then, just as Shelley slipped her glasses back on, the door to the conference room swung open, revealing both Hammett and Nurse Maidenkirk.

"Good morning, operatives," the pretend nurse offered stiffly, holding a tray piled high with chocolate, doughnuts, and maple syrup candies.

"We thought reinforcements might be needed in case you guys weren't feeling tip-top after only a few hours of sleep," Hammett explained as Nurse Maidenkirk placed the tray on the conference table.

"Felix and I require very little sleep. We can easily make do on two hours," Vera crowed.

"We can also sleep standing up if necessary. It's a preventative measure taken when resting in dangerous environments. For much like a zebra on the plains of Africa, we too respond faster to a predator if we're already standing," Felix added.

"Good to know, kid. Although personally, I prefer to do my sleeping in a bed with a pillow and a blanket," Hammett joshed, his trusty toothpick bobbing up and down in his mouth. "I spoke to the president this morning. He's concerned. Very concerned. Vice President Felinter's resistance must be worn thin by now. Plus, Mrs. Felinter is becoming semihysterical, having been unable to reach her husband during his Scandinavia trip."

"Mrs. Felinter has always liked to talk, mostly about flower arrangements and who knows the best dry cleaner," Nurse Maidenkirk interjected.

"Bottom line, that dame Felinter has a mouth big enough to sink the *Titanic*. She couldn't keep a secret if her life depended on it and certainly not if her husband's life depended on it," Hammett said as he stood up and started pacing back and forth behind his chair. "I wish I could tell you that life is fair, that the good guys always win, but we all know that's not true."

"You needn't worry, Hammett, we won't let the bad guys win, not this time," Vera stated confidently.

"Neither will we!" Shelley chimed in.

"Good. Now, we've received word that Gupta Nevers usually leaves his house around nine a.m. on

Saturdays for a soccer game in the park, so Vera and Felix, you are to pick up his tail as he leaves the house. Watch him carefully. Photograph everything. Leave nothing to chance," Hammett said as he flipped open a notebook and scanned a piece of paper. "Gupta lives alone except for a pet hamster named Clinton."

"I once had a hamster," Nurse Maidenkirk added.

Shelley rolled her eyes and then muttered, "Let me guess, he died."

"You are correct. He's dead. My cat ate him. All of him, even his fur."

Ignoring Nurse Maidenkirk, Hammett turned to Jonathan and Shelley. "Regarding your mission—"

"Not so fast, Hammett. I'd like to know why we haven't been given spy flies," Shelley inquired, glaring at the man over the top of her round-framed glasses.

"We've found that complicated gadgets do not mix well with unexceptionals. Plus, you guys don't need them. You've got the best tool there is—the ability to blend in. Now then, back to the mission—"

"More like babysitting job." Shelley bristled.

"Secretary of State Harold Foster is known to spend his weekends with his wife, Rita, and their eleven-year-old son, Jeffrey. Rita is a stay-at-home mom who enjoys baking apple pies, watching reality TV, and writing anonymous but very mean-spirited messages on parenting chat boards. Jeffrey is a cello prodigy who attends the Metropolitan School for Music."

"Jeffrey Foster? He went to elementary school with me. He called me Langdon or Louis. And I'm pretty sure he once hit me over the head with the bow of his cello," Jonathan reminisced.

"I can only imagine how difficult it is for you to protect yourself," Felix offered. "Of course, as Vera and I are black belts in Krav Maga, it's hard for us to relate."

"He totally made that word up," Shelley whispered rather loudly to Jonathan.

"Krav Maga is a type of self-defense that was developed in Israel," Vera explained.

After brushing the blond locks off his forehead, Felix added, "In Hebrew, *Krav* means 'battle' and *Maga* means 'contact.'"

Shelley tightened her jaw and muttered, "I'm about to Krav Maga them both in the head."

"I've been eating three bowls of blueberries, aka brain food, a day for the last six months and I still don't understand algebra."

—Simone T. Baxter, 15, Chubbuck, Idaho

CHAPTER 13

<087392-SB-LOUC-265>

OCTOBER 17, 8:15 A.M. FAMOUS RANDY'S
HOT DOG PALACE. WASHINGTON, DC

"May you have a better day than your astrological forecasts predict," Nurse Maidenkirk stated as Vera, Felix, Jonathan, and Shelley stood in front of Famous Randy's Hot Dog Palace.

Shelley shook her head. "I don't believe in horoscopes unless they contain good news, so if today's stinks, then it must not be true."

"You assume that good news is true and bad

news is false? How terribly unscientific of you," Vera remarked with a brief roll of the eyes.

"Shelley doesn't claim to be a scientist. A break-dancer, yes. But a scientist, never," Jonathan defended his partner.

"You know how to break-dance?" Felix asked with a twinge of envy.

This was the first thing Shelley knew that Felix did not, and the boy was not enjoying the sensation. Not one bit.

"What can I tell you, *Fel*," Shelley said, and then paused, shaking her head. "*Felix* just doesn't lend itself to nicknames, does it? Anyway, it's kind of a crazy story, but it all started with a garage sale. I bought a book on break-dancing for a quarter and boom, fourteen months later I posted a video of my signature moves and it went viral."

"Shelley, your video was viewed seven times, six of which were by you. The seventh, along with the comment 'I hope you lose a vital organ,' was tracked to your cousin Philomena Ward. But we really haven't time for such conversations." Nurse Maidenkirk bristled. "You have much to do if we stand any chance of finding the Seal before the vice president caves."

Vera pulled her left foot to her back in an impressive stretch. "We're running to Gupta's house. It's about two miles, so we'll make it in just under ten minutes."

"How funny! We're running to our destination too," Shelley bluffed as she did a very poor imitation of Vera's stretch.

"I'm not running anywhere. I have unforgiving calves; they don't respond well to extreme physical exercise," Jonathan mumbled.

"There's a blue sedan parked halfway down the block on the left side of the street. No ifs, ands, or buts, just get in," Nurse Maidenkirk ordered Jonathan and Shelley, and then walked back into Famous Randy's Hot Dog Palace as Vera and Felix sprinted off.

"You know why I hate her, don't you?" Shelley asked as she turned to face Jonathan.

"Who? Vera?"

"Yes Vera!" Shelley answered impatiently.

"Is it because she has a British accent and you don't?"

"No! Although, I could really rock that accent—"

"Please at least try to stay on track here," Jonathan interrupted.

"Vera is a walking reminder that life is not fair. She has shiny hair. I have dull hair. She's tall. I'm short. She's smart. I'm...well...not as smart. She's photogenic. I've had my picture omitted twice from the yearbook as a so-called act of kindness," Shelley ranted, her cheeks bright red.

"I'm beginning to think Nurse Maidenkirk's horoscope was right after all...."

OCTOBER 17, 8:58 A.M. EVANSTON, VIRGINIA

"Do you think we look suspicious? I mean, how many twelve-year-olds spend their Saturday mornings on a bench reading the *Washington Chronicle*?" Jonathan asked Shelley as the two sat beneath a tree approximately sixty feet up the street from Secretary of State Harold Foster's house in Evanston, Virginia.

"Well, it's either this or sit in the car with Mr. Moody over there," Shelley said as she motioned to Arthur Pelton seated in a sedan parked about twenty feet away.

"Poor guy, none of his clothes fit him properly. Even in jeans and a sweater he looks uncomfortable," Jonathan remarked.

"I'm so hungry....Just looking at this Cookie Monster guy, Alan Feith," Shelley said while glancing at the newspaper, "makes my stomach hurt. He's literally covered in crumbs...."

"Jeffrey's on the move," Jonathan interjected.

Shelley flipped her head and then squinted. "He appears to be taking the dog for a walk. Pretty suspicious, right?"

"Hardly," Jonathan said with a sigh. "Although Jeffrey's not very gentle with the dog. Look at the way he's yanking on the leash."

"I bet Vera and Felix are hanging from rafters taking pictures of Gupta while we're waiting for a dog to take a poo," Shelley huffed as Jeffrey returned home with the Labrador in tow.

A glimpse of red, seen out of the corner of his eye, suddenly grabbed Jonathan's attention. "Uh-oh, we have company."

Shelley looked up, shook her head, and plastered a phony smile across her face. "This is bad, very bad."

"Just try and act natural," Jonathan whispered.

"I am!"

"You're smiling like the Joker!"

"That's how people smile in Evanston," Shelley

retorted through clenched teeth as a woman on a bicycle with a large red flag pulled up in front of them.

"Good morning, children. My name is Mrs. Malins and I'm from Evanston's Community Patrol."

"Mrs. Malins, it's me, Shelley Brown, Carla and Gerald's granddaughter. You know, the one who's not a genius..."

But as usual, Mrs. Malins didn't hear Shelley and so the woman carried on. "I'm going to need to ask you two a few questions, starting with what brought you to Evanston today?"

"We live here," Jonathan answered.

"You live here?" Mrs. Malins repeated. "That trick may work in other towns, young man, but not here. In Evanston, we know our own."

"It's not a trick," Shelley said, standing up to get the woman's attention. "We go to Evanston Middle School."

Mrs. Malins looked Jonathan and Shelley up and down while narrowing her eyes.

"You're hooligans, aren't you? Here to write graffiti all over our clean walls! Well, I won't have it!"

Just then a black SUV stopped in front of the Foster residence and a Secret Service agent dressed in a suit exited the front seat. The man was medium sized with broad shoulders and a rather severe-looking scowl, the kind of expression that seamlessly communicated: "I will not hesitate to shoot."

"We need to get in the car," Jonathan instructed Shelley. "It looks like someone's on the move."

"I am not done with you!" Mrs. Malins hollered as she followed the two kids to the sedan. "Who is this man? Your father?"

"Our father? No. We are not related to each other and we are *definitely* not related to him," Shelley declared strongly.

"Then who is he?" Mrs. Malins inquired.

"He's a friend," Shelley lied as she and Jonathan jumped into the car.

Arthur Pelton, seemingly oblivious to Mrs. Malins, revved his engine, sending plumes of black smoke out the tailpipe.

"That, sir, is a serious infraction!" Mrs. Malins shouted as she tapped on Arthur Pelton's window. "I'm afraid I'm going to need to write you up!"

Harold, Rita, and Jeffrey Foster exited their home right as Mrs. Malins pulled out her ticket book.

"Hit the gas!" Shelley yelled at Arthur as the Fosters' black SUV pulled away.

"Not so fast!" Mrs. Malins screamed as she jumped on her bicycle, popped a flashing light on her helmet, and took off after the blue sedan.

OCTOBER 17, 9:35 A.M. ON THE ROAD. EVAN-STON, VIRGINIA

"Pull over! Right this second. You are in violation of at least three ordinances!" Mrs. Malins shouted while riding alongside the car.

"I don't want whatever you're selling," Arthur grunted, and then threw an old hamburger wrapper out the window at Mrs. Malins.

"Make that four ordinances! Littering is a serious crime in Evanston!"

"Can we please lose the trash police?" Shelley yelled, all the while keeping her eye on the black SUV two cars ahead.

"How am I supposed to do that, Miss Backseat Driver? If I go any faster, I'll smash into the car in front of me!"

"Pull over! I'm calling the police!" Mrs. Malins screamed.

"It's against Evanston Community Patrol regulations to talk on a cell phone while riding a bike," Jonathan pointed out. "She'll never do it."

"I don't know," Shelley remarked. "Look at her—she seems pretty serious."

"I have memorized your license plate! You will be permanently banned from entering Evanston ever again! Do you hear me?"

"The whole darn town hears you! Now will you leave us alone! We're trying to spy on someone!" Arthur raged, banging his pink hands on the steering wheel.

"You're not supposed to tell people we're spying! It's the first rule of being a spy," Shelley chastised him. "You're losing the SUV! You need to pass this car!"

"You're now three miles over the speed limit! If you injure a squirrel, I will hold you personally responsible for the vet bills," Mrs. Malins shrieked.

"Pass the car, but please try not to crash. Crashing brings a lot of unwanted attention," Jonathan advised Arthur as he overtook a red sedan, losing Mrs. Malins in the process.

"Where are the Fosters? We lost the Fosters!" Shelley exploded as she desperately looked for a glimpse of the SUV.

"They're in the parking lot of Southern Kitchen!" Jonathan screamed as Arthur crossed two lanes of traffic, shot over three speed bumps, and finally slammed on the brakes in front of the restaurant.

"This place makes the best fried chicken," Arthur said as he undid his seat belt and got out of the car.

"I guess that means he's coming with us," Shelley whispered under her breath.

"I realize that no one has ever remembered us, but I feel like that's about to change with Mrs. Malins," Jonathan said as he looked over his shoulder for either sight or sound of Community Patrol.

Before they had even opened the doors, the scent of syrup and barbecue sauce wafted past them, igniting rumbles from Shelley's stomach. And though they entered a few minutes after the secretary of state and his security entourage, whispers of excitement were still flickering around the room.

"I need to sit down. Car chases aren't for me," Jonathan moaned as he grabbed a chair at the closest unoccupied table.

"Let's not get carried away, it was a car chase with a bicycle. That's one small step above being chased by a poodle," Shelley remarked, watching the Fosters peruse their menus surrounded by Secret Service agents.

"I hate poodles almost as much as seals," Arthur groaned. "They think they're so special because they go to the hairdresser."

"Here we go again," Jonathan mumbled as a waiter approached the Foster table only to be patted down by Secret Service agents.

"Check it out, Secretary of State Foster is harder to talk to than Jason Heyman, who, by the way, once bumped into me in the hallway—I fell and skinned my knee but it was totally worth it," Shelley recalled, and then refocused her attention on the Fosters.

"Jeffrey hasn't changed much since elementary school," Jonathan assessed as he watched the boy ram his shoulder into a Secret Service agent's waist as he walked away from the table. "Interesting, the agents don't follow Jeffrey."

"They're probably hoping someone grabs him; he's such a menace," Shelley joked.

"Who? The Seal! You don't have to tell me that. I swear, if I ever get my hands on that guy, I'm going to bend down, grab him, and swing him around until he's begging for mercy!" Arthur growled, sweat dripping down his face.

"That's quite an image," Shelley said, and then paused. "What do you mean *bend down*?"

"The Seal is a tough-looking man, but he's short," Arthur explained.

"But neither Gupta Nevers nor Harold Foster is short," Jonathan said as he checked their profiles in *How to Make Great Popcorn in the Microwave*.

"No one could pull off something like this without help. Whoever is behind this obviously hired a short guy to do the kidnapping," Shelley speculated.

Jonathan nodded and then turned his attention back to Arthur. "What else do you remember about the Seal?"

"Not a lot. Only that he hated the Met Chil Phil too."

"The what?" Shelley asked.

"The Metropolitan Children's Philharmonic. They were playing their annual concert that night.

He said they were nothing but a bunch of ingrates," Arthur recalled. "I remember because I had to look up that word. And I hate looking up words!"

"Jeffrey's back," Shelley interrupted as she watched the boy return to the table, stepping on multiple Secret Service agents' feet along the way.

OCTOBER 17, 1:39 P.M. THE SMITHSONIAN MUSEUM. WASHINGTON, DC

"For the last time, you can't touch any of the art, especially not the paintings," Shelley reprimanded Arthur Pelton while trailing the Foster family, as well as the requisite Secret Service agents, through the Smithsonian.

"What kind of a museum doesn't let the visitors touch the artwork? I've never heard of such a thing," Arthur fumed. "What? Do they think I don't wash my hands? That I'm some kind of animal? Man, do I hate museums!"

"Oh, brother. First seals, then poodles, and now museums," Shelley muttered to herself as the Foster family turned into a small exhibition room.

"This thing hurts my eyes. It's just a bunch of

spots," Arthur huffed as he, Jonathan, and Shelley pretended to be absorbed in an unusual sculpture.

"The menace is on the move," Shelley whispered as the Foster family left the exhibition room.

"Who's the menace?" Arthur squawked loudly.

"Shh!" Jonathan and Shelley hushed the rotund man before popping in to see what the Fosters had been looking at—the world's most expensive cello, a Stradivarius dating from the eighteenth century. So renowned was the instrument that before being purchased by the Smithsonian, it had passed through the hands of British monarchs and Russian czars.

"What's with the big violin? You'd have to be a giant to play that," Arthur remarked.

At least there was one upside to hanging out with Arthur Pelton: He made Jonathan and Shelley feel smart—like geniuses, actually.

"Come on, we need to stay on the Fosters' tail," Jonathan said, and then turned to leave. Standing directly in front of him was a tall, gangly teenage boy holding a copy of *How to Make Great Popcorn in the Microwave*.

Shelley and Jonathan immediately froze, mouths agape. They stared at the boy. They stared at his book. But they didn't know what any of it meant and they most certainly didn't know how to handle the situation. And so they simply kept walking.

"Excuse me," the boy said as he squeezed past Jonathan, dropping something into his pocket.

"Only in New York City is
being average something
special."

—Lulu Bartholomew, 13,
New York City

OCTOBER 17, 2:29 P.M. THE SMITHSONIAN.
WASHINGTON, DC

Jonathan and Shelley walked warily down the corridor, the hairs on the back of their necks standing on edge. Their stomachs turned. Their mouths dried up. Their knees shook. Meanwhile, Arthur Pelton hadn't noticed a thing. He was waddling comfortably down the hall completely oblivious to what had transpired.

"I thought all League operatives were grounded,"

Shelley whispered. "Do you think he was an imposter? Has the Seal made us?"

"I have no clue. He could be an imposter or he could be an agent. The only thing I know for sure is that he dropped something in my pocket," Jonathan said to Shelley as she turned once again to confirm that the boy wasn't following them.

"Well, what is it?" Shelley asked, her voice dry and raspy from nerves.

Jonathan pushed the hair off his forehead and sighed. He knew he had to drop his fingers into his pocket and yet he waited. He waited as if somehow, some way, it would become easier. That he would stop wondering whether it might be something dangerous like a baby rattlesnake. Or a razor blade.

"Come on, Johno," Shelley urged.

"I'm doing it," Jonathan grumbled as he pushed his left hand into his pocket, forcing his fingers to graze the smooth cylinder-shaped item.

"Johno, this isn't a contest to see if you can guess what it is without looking, so please just pull it out," Shelley complained impatiently.

And so he did. It was a jalapeño.

Shelley removed her glasses and shook her head. "He put a pepper in your pocket? Now that's just weird."

"You still haven't read *How to Make Great Popcorn in the Microwave*?" Jonathan moaned.

"I know it's not actually about popcorn, but it just sounds so boring," Shelley explained.

"A jalapeño means there's an emergency...."

"The VP!" Shelley yelped. "The Seal finally broke him!"

OCTOBER 17, 3:03 P.M. THE SMITHSONIAN. WASHINGTON, DC

Jonathan, Shelley, and Arthur Pelton had only just exited the museum when they spotted Hammett pacing a few feet away.

"We've got a situation on our hands, kiddos. We need to move now!" Hammett instructed Jonathan and Shelley, and then turned to Arthur. "Here's a fiver, go get yourself an ice cream."

"But I'm lactose intolerant."

"Then make it a sorbet!"

As Arthur walked away, Hammett ushered

Jonathan and Shelley off the Mall to an idling 1970s black Cadillac with Nurse Maidenkirk behind the wheel.

Hammett threw open the heavy door. "Get in."

OCTOBER 17, 3:12 P.M. ON THE MOVE. WASHINGTON, DC

Squeezed into the backseat between Vera and Felix, Jonathan and Shelley exchanged confused looks. The car rattled and squeaked at every bump and crack in the road. It was an old car, but to Jonathan it felt more like a boat. It swayed and rocked, leaving him queasy. He wanted to scream "Pull over," but he couldn't. Something big was happening, something more important than a twelve-year-old's car sickness.

"Here's the deal: Vice President Felinter woke up in a Dumpster on the south side of town this morning. He was covered in black trash bags, old food, and items that I'd rather not say. He doesn't know where he was kept the last few days and he never got a good look at his captor. Bottom line, he's pretty much as useless as ever," Hammett expounded.

"The Seal wouldn't have let the vice president go without the code, so I assume he now has access to the mainframe," Vera said solemnly.

"We don't know that he caved; have a little faith," Shelley said, more because she wanted to disagree with Vera than because she actually believed it.

"Unfortunately, Vice President Felinter caved like an old mine shaft in an earthquake," Hammett interjected. "He wrote down the second code yesterday and this morning he woke up in the trash, literally."

"Then what are we doing here? Just waiting for the documents to come out and the country to crumble?" Jonathan asked.

"It's not quite over yet. We have one last chance to stop the Seal before the documents get out," Hammett explained. "The vice president heard the Seal whispering about meeting someone for the handoff on Tuesday."

"Which means we have a little more than two days to identify the Seal and stop the exchange," Nurse Maidenkirk added as she pulled the car in front of a redbrick building on New York Avenue.

OCTOBER 17, 3:20 P.M. THE OCTAGON HOUSE.
WASHINGTON, DC

"This is the Octagon House, one of Washington's *least* famous museums, but an important one nonetheless. Presidents have stayed here, treaties have been signed here—"

"But what are we doing here?" Vera interrupted Nurse Maidenkirk. "We only have a few days to figure out whether the Seal is Gupta Nevers or Harold Foster. We need to be trailing them, not visiting the sights in DC."

"Jonathan and Shelley are meeting Vice President Felinter inside. If he can remember anything, even if it's something small, it could help us," Hammett said as Vera rolled her eyes and released a Jonathan-worthy sigh.

"You're sending *them* in? What about us?" Felix protested.

"Don't call us *them*!" Shelley snapped.

"Vera, Felix—you're too noticeable. You look like models, and people remember models," Hammett explained.

"Then why did you bring us here? We could be

shadowing Gupta," Vera said in a rather prickly tone of voice.

"Jonathan and Shelley blend well, but they're new. They're inexperienced. If something goes wrong, we're going to need backup to rescue them," Hammett answered.

"Do you have to use the word *rescue*? It's not much of a confidence builder," Jonathan mumbled.

"Vice President Felinter is undercover, dressed as a tourist with a fanny pack and all. I need you to question him, see if he remembers anything," Hammett instructed, and then motioned for Jonathan and Shelley to exit.

"Enjoy the car, tacos.... I'm not really sure why I called you tacos; it just slipped out. Although, I do really like tacos," Shelley babbled to Vera and Felix as she and Jonathan climbed out of the enormous black Cadillac.

The Octagon House was a traditional redbrick building dating from the early 1800s, three stories tall, and impeccably maintained. Jonathan and Shelley crossed the sidewalk and mounted the few steps leading to the building's dark brown door.

"Welcome to the Octagon House! Admission is free, although we do accept donations," said a bald man with thick Coke-bottle glasses, no older than fifty, as the two entered the building's lobby.

"No problem. I've always been very charitable," Shelley said before dropping something shiny into a jar and moving toward the imposing staircase that wrapped around each of the three floors.

"I would have given him some change, but I only have bills. And donating a dollar is kind of steep for a twelve-year-old," Jonathan whispered to Shelley as they started upstairs.

"Don't worry, I totally get it," Shelley mumbled. "You're cheap."

"What? No!" Jonathan responded.

"Shh, we're in a museum."

"I'm not cheap, I'm responsible. There's a big difference!"

"Fine, whatever you say, big spender, just lower your voice, we're working here," Shelley reprimanded Jonathan as the two stepped onto the second floor.

"Straight ahead," Jonathan whispered upon seeing a tall man in a baseball cap, jeans, sneakers, and most important, a fanny pack.

"This is it, Johno, this is the moment our lives finally become interesting."

"Shelley, we're spies. We were kidnapped and tossed out of a van with burlap sacks on our heads. We regularly crawl through a pork-filled refrigerator to get to headquarters. I think we can both agree, our lives are *already* interesting."

"That was the nicest thing you've ever said to me," Shelley said, and then threw her arms around Jonathan, causing him to blush.

"There's no hugging in espionage—be professional," Jonathan mumbled as he started toward the man with the fanny pack.

"Excuse me, sir?" Jonathan called out, prompting the man to turn around.

"Yeah?"

"Are you here on a vacation?" Shelley asked, raising her eyebrows.

"What did you say? You're going to have to speak up, little lady."

"I said, are you here on vacation?" Shelley repeated loudly.

"In DC? I sure am."

"So you're a tourist?" Jonathan asked.

"Yeah, I'm a tourist. What's this about? Is the government taxing tourists now?"

"I think you know what this is about," Shelley declared pointedly as she stepped closer to the man.

"Pardon? I'm having a real hard time hearing you," the man told Shelley as he leaned down.

"You're really working your cover," Shelley said, staring at the man over the top of her glasses. "I get it. You want to fully vet us before you spill the beans."

"What did you say about a vet? Is an animal hurt?"

"Why don't I take over; he clearly has some hearing issues," Jonathan whispered.

"No." Shelley bristled. "You're not blocking me from being a part of history! This is something I'm going to tell my grandkids about!"

"Actually, it's not. It's top secret. Everything we do for League is confidential," Jonathan reminded Shelley.

"You always were a buzzkill."

"I don't mean to be rude, but like I said, I'm on vacation," the man explained as he started to walk away.

"Not so fast, fanny pack!" Shelley barked. "The future of this country could depend on what you tell us, so cut the act and give us the info."

"What did you call me?" the man asked.

"You heard me, *fanny pack*!" Shelley replied angrily.

"Something doesn't feel right here....Abort... abort..." Jonathan muttered as he stared at the man's genuinely confused face. "There's no way the VP is this good an actor."

"Oh, it's him all right," Shelley declared. "I can see the glue on his mustache from here."

She then lunged at the man, grabbed hold of the strip of thick brown hair on his upper lip, and pulled with all her might.

"AHHHHHH!!!!!" the man shrieked as his face turned beet red.

"Shelley, it's not HIM! Let go!"

Having realized that she just attacked an innocent man and attempted to rip out his facial hair, Shelley lowered her head in shame. "I'm sorry."

"There's not much I can say other than my friend is crazy," Jonathan said solemnly as the man with the fanny pack turned and exited the room, all the while shaking his head in disbelief.

"I guess fanny packs are making a comeback," Shelley said sheepishly. "It never occurred to me that someone would wear one of those for fun."

"Come on, we need to find the VP," Jonathan said as he ushered Shelley into the next room.

Unfortunately, after thirty minutes, they had yet to see another person. The museum was literally empty.

"Maybe he had to cancel?" Jonathan supposed as they made their way down the staircase to the lobby.

"Excuse me," the bald docent called out as they passed the front desk. "But we don't accept gum wrappers as donations."

"Fine, whatever! I'm not in the mood!"

"You put a gum wrapper in the jar? And to think, you called me cheap," Jonathan scolded Shelley.

The docent stood up from behind the desk, revealing a large and incredibly ugly fanny pack. Bulky, made of green-and-yellow fabric that crinkled when he moved, it was an absolute eyesore.

"I wanted to grab you on the way in, but I was worried the man upstairs might be listening," the docent explained.

"It's a pleasure to meet you, sir," Jonathan offered sincerely, extending his hand to shake.

"Johno, it's not him. Trust me. I'd know Carl if I saw him," Shelley said with a sense of authority that Jonathan didn't quite understand.

"Don't call him Carl like he's your old friend. Show some respect."

"It's not him, Johno," Shelley stated emphatically.

"Shells, you thought that random guy upstairs was our target, so excuse me for not trusting your instincts," Jonathan shot back.

"No need to argue," the docent said. "I'm Carl."

"You're Carl?" Shelley repeated. "Like *the Carl*."

"Stop calling him Carl!" Jonathan snapped, and then turned to the vice president. "We don't have much time, sir; is there anything you can tell us about the Seal or where you were kept?"

"Not a whole lot," Carl replied. "The walls were padded. He fed me potato chips and candy bars. He was ruthless. He plucked my nose hairs one at a time until there were none left, then he moved on to my ears."

"I'm sorry, sir. That sounds dreadful," Jonathan commiserated.

"I wish I could be of more help. But the only useful thing I heard was that he's meeting the buyer on Tuesday," the vice president said, and then dropped his face into his hands. "I let my country down."

"It's not over yet," Shelley declared, and then held up her hand for a high five. "What? You're not feeling the high five? How about a hug?"

"Do not hug the vice president," Jonathan reprimanded Shelley.

"Actually, I could use a hug."

And so Shelley Brown hugged the vice president of the United States—definitely a moment worthy of her memoir.

TOP SECRET

"The only thing I've ever been good at is *not* being good at anything."

—Jim Schulty, 12,
Boulder, Colorado

SECURE DOCUMENTS

CHAPTER 15

<067982-JS-LOUC-976>

Sunday was an unremarkable day. The sun stayed hidden behind a scattering of clouds. The wind blew lightly. Leaves fell to the ground. It was the kind of day that blended into a million others. But not for Jonathan Murray and Shelley Brown. This was the day they passed fifteen hours on a bench in Evanston, Virginia, staring at a house, waiting for someone, anyone, in the Foster family to leave. But they never did, not even to walk the dog. In fact, the only human interaction Jonathan or Shelley had came in the form of Mrs. Malins from Community Patrol, who was passing out fliers featuring an impressively accurate sketch of Arthur. And though it worked to their advantage, Jonathan and Shelley couldn't help but feel miffed at the flier's small print "last seen in the company of two *nondescript* children."

OCTOBER 19, 6:32 A.M. EVANSTON, VIRGINIA

After the failure of the previous day's mission, Jonathan and Shelley had realized they needed a new plan. There was no longer time to simply watch Secretary of State Harold Foster from afar. They had one day left before the Seal sold the documents, and they were determined to make it count, especially since Vera and Felix's failure to uncover anything incriminating on Gupta Nevers meant that no one could be ruled out.

Just past six thirty in the morning, Jonathan pushed back his plain white sheets, wiped the sleep from his eyes, and took a deep breath. He didn't feel ready for what lay ahead, but he also knew that he would never feel ready. And so the boy showered, brushed his teeth, and dressed, only this time he decided to try something a little different. This time Jonathan Murray put on a pair of jeans. They were stiff and uncomfortable. He looked at himself in the mirror; he felt younger, more like a kid. Maybe he didn't need his khakis as much as before. He had always worn them because they set him apart from his parents. They told the world that unlike Carmen and Mickey, Jonathan would always maintain a respectable lawn. But somehow, after everything that had transpired, Jonathan was no longer afraid that he would turn into his parents. For if there was one thing he had learned, the future couldn't be predicted. After all, it was only a week ago that he was a boring, dull kid walking aimlessly through life. And yet today, he was a member of the League of Unexceptional Children, tasked with saving his country.

Jonathan slipped out the front door and walked the two blocks to Shelley's grandparents' place, a house as perfect and well manicured as any other in Evanston. It was the kind of place that used to make Jonathan jealous; he had always wanted a well-painted home. But as his last chance to stop the Seal fast approached, he realized how little such things mattered.

"Johno," Shelley called out as the garage door opened. "What do you want, wind or strings?"

"What did you choose?"

"The trumpet," Shelley answered.

"Then I'll take the violin."

Seconds later Shelley exited the garage with two hard black cases. However, upon seeing Jonathan, Shelley quickly dropped to the ground.

"I don't feel so well...."

"What is it?" Jonathan asked as he hurried to his friend's side.

"I'm hallucinating.... Your khakis look like jeans," Shelley said, and then broke into a fit of laughter.

"Very funny," Jonathan responded as Shelley handed him one of the black cases.

"Your sister can really play both the trumpet and the violin?"

"She's basically a one-woman band. Pretty impressive, right?"

"It's okay"—Jonathan shrugged—"but it's not like she's a spy or anything."

OCTOBER 19, 7:42 A.M. THE METRO. WASH-
INGTON, DC

Jonathan and Shelley marched up the stairs
of the Metro and into the heart of the District of
Columbia. They walked with the confidence of
Vera and Felix. And not because they knew what
they were doing. They most definitely did not
know what they were doing. But this was their last
chance to get close to the secretary of state, to see if
he was the Seal, and they were determined to give
it their all.

The Metropolitan School for Music was not
nearly as clean or impressive-looking as Evanston
Middle School, nor was there classical music pip-
ing out of every corner or organic food carts in the
cafeteria. It was a city school spread over four lev-
els, the halls positively crawling with students and
instruments.

"I was thinking maybe we should try out some
new first names. Veronica? Vladimir? Aretha?
Frank?" Shelley proposed as the two walked down
a crowded corridor.

"Shells, Hammett said to use our own first
names. Plus, I think it's best we don't overcompli-
cate things."

"I take it that means you want to skip the
accents too?"

"Let's leave the accents to Vera and Felix and
just focus on Jeffrey."

"I'm sure if we listen carefully, we can follow the
sound of his classmates' screams," Shelley said.

"He's not that bad."

"Jeffrey kicked a Secret Service agent in the shin and then laughed," Shelley reminded Jonathan.

"Admittedly, he's not the most charming or gentle of children. But we need to find a way to relate to the little barbarian," Jonathan said as he pulled out his copy of *How to Make Great Popcorn in the Microwave*. "Come on, he has English first period. And remember, no accents, no limps, no fake first names."

"No problem. Shells is all bells, which means she won't ring unless...uh...you know what?"

Jonathan held up his hand. "No need to even ask, the statement has already been retracted."

Shelley and Jonathan sat smack dab in the middle of the classroom. Not that anyone looked at them or questioned them. On the contrary, the students and teachers didn't even notice them. It was as if their chairs were empty.

"There he is," Jonathan whispered as Jeffrey marched into the classroom, knocking his backpack against another student's desk, sending her folder to the floor.

"Where's Mr. Nelson? I don't have all day to just sit around here," Jeffrey complained as a young teacher no more than thirty entered the room, bicycle helmet still on his head. "You're late, Mr. Nelson."

"My apologies, Mr. Foster, but there was an accident, and as a witness, I had a civic duty to stay and give my account to the police officers," Mr. Nelson explained as he removed his helmet and dropped his bag.

Throughout the period Jeffrey argued relentlessly with his teacher, challenging his every statement. So much so that by the time the bell rang, Shelley and Jonathan were so sick of the sound of Jeffrey's voice, they decided to hide out in one of the practice rooms in the basement until they could approach him at recess.

The Metropolitan School for Music's basement was a sorry affair. It was dark, damp, and as such rarely used. Jonathan and Shelley tucked into one of the ten small square rooms whose walls were covered in foam to block the sound of students practicing their instruments.

Seated on the floor, with their backs against the wall, Shelley leaned in and whispered, "Tell me a secret."

"Why?"

"I'm bored. Plus, the world as we know it might fall apart, so what have we got to lose?" Shelley answered honestly.

Jonathan nodded and then sighed. "I guess I can't argue with that."

He then closed his eyes and racked his brain for something worthy of being called a secret. But it wasn't easy, for the boy had led a rather dull life, leaving him with few skeletons in his closet.

"I once bought a book called *How to Be Interesting*," Jonathan finally mumbled.

"Did it work?"

"Let me put it to you this way: Both of my parents fell asleep during my Thanksgiving toast last year," Jonathan answered seconds before the bell rang.

Upon exiting, the two made their way down the long vending machine–filled corridor to the staircase to the cafeteria.

"You remember your story?" Shelley asked Jonathan as the two covertly watched Jeffrey from across the lunchroom.

Seated alone at a table reading a magazine, Jeffrey emitted an unfriendly, that-seat-is-taken kind of vibe.

"Are you sure you don't want me to do the talking?" Shelley asked Jonathan as they approached.

"No, I have a legitimate backstory. We went to elementary school together for a few years. He even assaulted me."

"I know it's true, but it sort of sounds like a lie. I would go with something more believable, like band camp," Shelley advised.

"Band camp?" Jonathan repeated.

"No need to make that face, it was just an idea," Shelley said as Jonathan moved closer to Jeffrey's table.

Standing mere inches from the target, he felt his mouth dry up. He wanted to turn around and get a glass of water, but he knew he couldn't. Spies didn't stop for water breaks.

"Hey, you're Jeffrey Foster, right?" Jonathan asked.

"Who are you?"

"It's me...Jonathan...from band camp. I just transferred in with my sister, Shelley."

"How riveting," Jeffrey answered flatly, and then looked down at his magazine, effectively dismissing Jonathan from the table.

Unsure how to proceed, he turned and looked at Shelley, who motioned to continue with the conversation.

"Your solo last summer was—"

"I didn't have a solo last summer," Jeffrey corrected Jonathan harshly.

"Exactly. What I was going to say was your solo was *stolen* from you last summer."

"You got that right. But you know Mr. Plimpton, always trying to make everyone feel special, pretending that everyone's equal. What a load of garbage."

"Total garbage," Jonathan agreed. "Plimpton's the worst."

"Let me see your fingers."

Jonathan slowly presented his hands to the boy.

"Interesting. What instrument do you play?"

"The violin."

"But you don't have the fingers of a violinist," Jeffrey countered, prompting Jonathan to immediately start sweating.

"That's because I just switched to the violin from the saxophone," Jonathan fibbed, his mouth growing drier by the second.

"I hate wind instruments," Jeffrey growled.

"Me too. That's why I switched to the violin. I wanted to play the cello, but after hearing you last summer, I thought, Why even bother?"

"You were right; there's no reason to bother. I will always be the best," Jeffrey crowed, and then looked Jonathan up and down. "What are you doing after school? Do you want to come over and watch me play? I won't charge you."

"That sounds great, but can I bring my sister?"

"As long as she doesn't talk."

"No problem, she's basically a mute," Jonathan lied, amazed that Shelley hadn't already inserted herself into the conversation.

"Okay, Paul, meet me in front of the main hall after school. I'll be in the black SUV."

OCTOBER 19, 3:07 P.M. METROPOLITAN SCHOOL FOR MUSIC. WASHINGTON, DC

"Remember, he thinks my name is Paul," Jonathan reminded Shelley as the two exited the school.

"Of course he does."

"And no talking," Jonathan reiterated as he spotted the black SUV.

"What a shame," Shelley lamented. "My mouth is my greatest asset in espionage."

"You don't need to talk for the plan to work. I'm going to keep Jeffrey busy while you look around and see what you can find on his father."

"Fine," Shelley relented as the two approached the vehicle and then tapped lightly on the tinted glass.

Jeffrey rolled down the window and removed his sunglasses.

"Paul, you and your sister need to sit in the back. This row's only for me and my cello," Jeffrey stated, and then promptly rolled up the window.

"Why don't we just ride in the trunk?" Shelley muttered under her breath as the two climbed into the highly claustrophobic third row.

Jeffrey didn't speak for the entire car ride home. He didn't speak to the driver and he didn't speak to Shelley or Jonathan. He just sat there next to his cello.

OCTOBER 19, 3:43 P.M. EVANSTON, VIRGINIA

Upon arriving at the Foster residence, Jeffrey grabbed his cello and marched straight inside, without so much as looking back at his guests.

"Nice digs," Shelley said as she entered, Jonathan immediately behind her.

"Follow me, Paul. I want to play something new for you," Jeffrey ordered. "You too, Smelly."

"Did you just call me Smelly?" Shelley asked incredulously.

"I did," Jeffrey shot back. "And?"

Jonathan stared at Shelley, silently reminding her of what was at stake.

"And nothing. My name is Smelly...Smelly Smith."

Jeffrey's room was large; the walls covered with posters of the world's greatest cellists—Yo-Yo Ma, Jacqueline du Pré, Mstislav Rostropovich, and so on.

"Silence your phone. And do not clap until I'm done," Jeffrey said as Jonathan took a seat.

"You met the president?" Shelley asked, looking at a photo of Jeffrey and Max Arons in front of the White House.

"I thought you said she was mute!"

"Sorry," Jonathan muttered. "Come on, Smelly, try and keep it down, would you?"

"No problem, Paul," Shelley replied, and then turned to Jeffrey. "Can I use your bathroom?"

"Second door on the left," the boy grunted before picking up his bow and starting to play.

Tiptoeing through the house, Shelley carefully pried open drawers, looked through papers, and generally just stuck her nose in places it most definitely did not belong. Thoughts of Vera drifted through her head as she fiddled with the pieces on a chessboard in the sitting area attached to the master bedroom. Who did Vera think she was? A genius? Ugh, she probably was a genius, Shelley thought as she knocked her knee against the coffee table, sending a book about talking in your sleep crashing to the floor.

Determined to find something on Secretary of State Harold Foster so she could help her country *and* show up Vera, Shelley peeked into the study. A large wooden desk and two wingback chairs filled the dimly lit room.

" 'Home is where the heart is'?" Shelley muttered, reading a needlepoint pillow displayed on one of the chairs. "That's not right....It's 'Home is where the car is'...because you only park your car at home.... Wait a minute, what's that?" she whispered upon noticing a thick leather address book on the desk.

Flipping through the pages, Shelley paused at familiar names—George W. Bush, Hillary Clinton, Alan Feith, Al Gore. Sensing a dead end, she quickly moved on to the collection of framed photographs behind the desk. The Foster family at the Grand Canyon. Jeffrey and the Metropolitan Children's Philharmonic. Rita and Harold at a fancy party. Frustrated with the lack of smoking guns, Shelley sighed and started back toward Jeffrey's room, popping into the bathroom along the way.

After inspecting a few mundane items in the medicine chest—a toothbrush, toothpaste, hair gel—Shelley opened a small black case containing a pair of stainless steel tweezers. Almost instantly her eyes widened, her mouth opened, and her hands trembled; images of the vice president's freshly plucked nostrils and the photo of Jeffrey with the Metropolitan Children's Philharmonic raced through her head.

"Sometimes I think my dog's judging me; he looks at me like, *Even I could have done better on that test.*"

—Jason McElroy, 11,
Tulsa, Oklahoma

CHAPTER 16

<098374-JM-LOUC-873>

OCTOBER 19, 4:16 P.M. EVANSTON, VIRGINIA
Upon hearing thunderous clapping from Jeffrey's room, Shelley opened the door. "Wow. Talk about a musical genius."

"I get that a lot."

"I mean you are *seriously* good. Like good enough to be in the Metropolitan Children's Philharmonic," Shelley continued.

"The Met Chil Phil is a joke!" Jeffrey fumed. "They are nothing but a bunch of talentless ingrates!"

"I'm sorry, but did you just call them ingrates?" Jonathan interjected.

"They didn't appreciate me while they had me. But they'll be sorry," Jeffrey said ominously.

"And on that note, I think we should be getting home," Shelley said as she and Jonathan started for the door.

"By the way," the boy said before returning to his cello, "my fan page is jeffreyfosterisagenius.com."

OCTOBER 19, 5:46 P.M. THE LEAGUE OF UNEXCEPTIONAL CHILDREN HEADQUARTERS. WASHINGTON, DC

Shelley and Jonathan paced excitedly back and forth in the conference room while Vera, Felix, Nurse Maidenkirk, and Hammett watched them carefully, hanging on their every word.

"Harold Foster is the Seal. And he used his son, Jeffrey, to pull this whole thing off," Jonathan stated, still awestruck by what the two had discovered.

"Jeffrey called the Metropolitan Children's Philharmonic 'ingrates,' which is the exact word the Seal used when talking to Arthur Pelton the night of the kidnapping," Shelley added.

"That could be nothing more than a coincidence," Felix offered dismissively.

"I also found a pair of stainless steel tweezers in Jeffrey's medicine cabinet," Shelley continued.

"So he tweezes, big deal, so do I," Vera chimed in.

"If Harold and Jeffrey took the vice president, where did they keep him?" Hammett wondered aloud.

"A practice room at the Metropolitan School for Music. The walls are padded and there are lots of vending machines, making it very easy to feed your hostage potato chips and candy bars," Jonathan expounded.

"No wonder we couldn't find anything on Gupta Nevers," Vera muttered to herself.

"That is not entirely accurate. You discovered that Gupta's hamster, Clinton, died," Nurse Maidenkirk responded. "And that his neighbor's dog dug up the body."

"Another great Maidenkirk story," Jonathan mumbled under his breath.

"If you guys don't mind, I'd like to take a moment to review the facts: Vera and Felix discovered a dead hamster. Jonathan and I revealed the identity of the man trying to bring down the United States government," Shelley stated smugly, and then bowed.

"I think bowing might be overkill," Jonathan whispered as she returned to a standing position.

Hammett pulled the toothpick from his mouth and stood up. "Tomorrow's D-day, kiddos. And to put it bluntly, none of this means a doggone thing unless we stop the Seal in time."

"Then let's go pick up the Fosters now," Felix suggested. "Vera and I are more than capable of bringing them in."

"Back off, Felix," Shelley snapped.

"No, the president wants us to wait," Hammett explained. "He doesn't just want the Seal, he wants the buyer too...."

OCTOBER 20, 8:09 A.M. EVANSTON, VIRGINIA

The wind whipped through the streets of Evanston, carrying the faint sound of bells and chattering voices. Jonathan and Shelley sat on the bench just up the way from the Fosters' residence. Stationed down the block, in his blue sedan, was Arthur Pelton. Across the street, crouched behind trash cans, Vera and Felix used their spy fly to peer through the windows.

"Jeffrey finished brushing his teeth; he's headed downstairs," Vera whispered into a microphone clipped to the cuff of her shirt while watching the video feed from the spy fly on her phone.

"Roger that," Shelley said, also into her cuff.

"Hammett seems pretty sure that Harold Foster will send Jeffrey for the drop, seeing as Harold's always surrounded by Secret Service agents," Jonathan stated as the receiver in his ear crackled.

"Jeffrey is on the move. I repeat, Jeffrey is on the move," Felix's voice buzzed.

"Oh no... What is he doing?" Shelley squealed upon spotting Arthur walking toward them.

"Please get back in the car," Jonathan begged as he simultaneously noted Jeffrey exiting the house.

"No way!" Arthur huffed. "You guys need me! I'm an adult!"

"We don't need you, like not even a little bit," Shelley responded as she watched Jeffrey walk down the block, occasionally stopping to swat at something in front of his face.

"You're getting too close with the spy fly," Jonathan whispered into his cuff. "Pull back."

"Do not tell us how to use the spy fly, unexceptionals." Vera bristled through the radio.

"We need to move," Shelley informed Jonathan as the two started down the street, Arthur waddling behind them.

"I will buy you a lifetime supply of hot dogs if you just go back to the car," Jonathan pleaded.

"Why on earth are you bringing the security guard along?" Felix asked over the radio as he and Vera started covertly following Jeffrey.

"We're trying our best to lose him. But it's not easy!" Shelley huffed.

"What's that smell?" Jonathan asked, covering his nose with his hand.

"Raw sardines. I brought them to lure the Seal," Arthur explained as he pulled a small silver fish from his pocket.

"You let the Seal into the White House, so you obviously know he isn't an *actual seal*," Shelley said, shaking her head.

"Yeah, but he's called the Seal, so he might like

fish too," Arthur answered as though it were the most logical of explanations.

"We have a problem," Vera announced over the radio. "According to the images picked up by the spy fly, Jeffrey turned the corner and walked straight into some kind of convention on the village green. The area is swarming with people on bicycles with red flags."

"Ugh, Evanston's Community Patrol! They're probably having their monthly meet-up," Shelley groaned as she and Jonathan started running, Arthur wheezing behind them.

Upon turning the corner, Shelley and Jonathan promptly froze. The village green, a grassy area in the middle of town, was overflowing with Community Patrol volunteers, all of whom were wearing red vests and name tags.

"We've lost sight of Jeffrey," Jonathan said into his cuff, short of breath from running.

"Not to worry, I have sardines," Arthur mumbled as he wiped his sleeve against his heavily perspiring forehead.

"Unexceptionals!" Vera called out from behind them. "How could you lose Jeffrey?"

"But aren't you following him with the spy fly?" Jonathan asked.

"One of those pesky people in the red vests smashed it with her hands, thinking it was an actual insect," Felix griped.

"We don't have much time. We need to locate Jeffrey before he makes the exchange. I'm not trying to scare you, but it's highly likely he's selling the nuclear codes," Vera stated gravely.

"The nuclear codes?" Arthur shrieked. "We're all going to die!"

Shelley shook her head. "Nice job, Vera. You freaked out the adult."

"There's no time for bickering," Jonathan interjected. "We need to break up and find Jeffrey! Now!"

"Vera and I will go right, you go left," Felix said as the two groups headed into the crowd, Arthur trailing behind Jonathan and Shelley.

"We need to pass proposition three point nine, unless of course you don't mind those ugly satellite dishes ruining the neighborhood."

"I think we should become a gated community— it's the only surefire way to keep out the riffraff," a woman from Community Patrol squawked and then paused upon seeing Arthur. "Do you remember that man from Mrs. Malins's flier? I think that's him!"

"I wish we could help, but there just isn't time," Jonathan remarked as he watched a slew of angry Community Patrol volunteers surround Arthur.

"Look at this place. Finding Jeffrey is going to be like finding a beetle in a haystack."

"A needle," Jonathan mumbled.

"Excuse me?"

"The saying is a *needle* in a haystack, not a *beetle*."

"That makes no sense! Who uses needles outside? Beetles, on the other hand, live outside and could easily get lost in a pile of hay!"

"Who cares about beetles? We need to think! Where would Jeffrey go?" Jonathan exclaimed as he heard the familiar sound of people being bumped and pushed.

"Ouch!"

"Watch where you're going!"

"Excuse me, but in Evanston we don't push! You can even look it up, ordinance nine point eight!"

"This way," Jonathan called to Shelley, and then whispered into his sleeve, "We think we've picked up Jeffrey's trail, headed toward the playground."

"Move those knees!" Vera shouted at Felix as the two sprinted across the green, desperate to catch up with Jonathan and Shelley. "Faster, Felix, faster! We can't let the unexceptionals capture the Seal without us!"

"Oh, the shame of losing to *them*!" Felix uttered as the two increased their pace. "We'd have to go into hiding."

Following the sound of complaints, Jonathan and Shelley finally caught sight of Jeffrey.

"There he is," Shelley said upon spotting the boy moving toward the children's playground.

"Wait a minute," Jonathan muttered as he caught a flash of something familiar in the crowd.

"What is it?" Shelley asked.

"That man over there…on the other side of the playground…the one with the crazy hair…" Jonathan said as he focused in on a tall, slender man with gray locks teased approximately six inches high.

"It's the Cookie Monster!" Shelley interrupted.

"You know, Alan Feith, the guy who's on trial for stealing all that money."

"He must be the buyer. Why else would he be here?" Jonathan supposed as he watched the man enter the playground.

"If you're right, we need to move fast!" Shelley stated as the two dove into a red plastic tunnel, then swung across monkey bars, and finally glided down a slide.

"I don't see them! Where are they?" Jonathan asked while frantically looking around the playground.

"They have to be here somewhere," Shelley mumbled.

"Shhh…" Jonathan whispered as he listened for even the faintest sound of Jeffrey or Alan.

"Look," Shelley exclaimed quietly as she noted a trail of cookie crumbs leading toward a large pyramid built out of black tractor-sized tires.

The two instantly started up the mountainlike structure, although Jonathan quickly fell behind Shelley.

"Keep going." Jonathan wheezed. "We can't let him sell the nuclear codes!"

"Not on my watch!" Shelley huffed as she clawed her way to the top of the pyramid and stealthily grabbed hold of the corner of Jeffrey's jeans.

"Hey! What are you doing?" the boy yelled, kicking his leg to loosen Shelley's grip, ultimately knocking her down.

"You set me up!" Alan Feith screamed at Jeffrey as the two started barreling down the pyramid.

"I was so close," Shelley whimpered as Jonathan grabbed her arm.

"Come on, Shells. This isn't over yet. If we're going to fail, let's at least fail big!"

Sweating, out of breath, and deeply red in the face, Jonathan and Shelley descended the pyramid.

"I don't see them," Shelley said, frantically scanning her surroundings.

"We need a better viewpoint," Jonathan assessed as he started to pull himself up the face of a tall and slippery slide.

After watching Jonathan struggle for a few seconds, Shelley walked to the back of the slide and quickly climbed the ladder to the top.

"I've got Jeffrey at three o'clock."

"I'm...coming...almost there..." Jonathan said in between gasps of air while fighting to make it up the face of the slide.

"You know what? Maybe it's more like two thirty...or four..." Shelley trailed off. "Oh, forget it! It doesn't matter, he's headed in our direction!"

"Jeffrey's going down," Jonathan whispered nearly inaudibly, after strenuously pulling himself atop the slide.

"You can say that again," Shelley muttered, then crouched down and waited.

Seconds passed. Jeffrey grew closer and closer until he was mere feet from the slide. After a quick wink to Jonathan, Shelley lunged from her perch, catapulted through the air, and knocked Jeffrey to the ground.

"That was awesome!" Jonathan shrieked as he slid down the slide and joined Shelley, who was wrestling Jeffrey for a small white piece of paper.

"You ruined everything!" the boy bellowed. "And now I'm going to ruin you!"

"Please, you don't even know my name!" Shelley scoffed as Jonathan pinned Jeffrey's left arm to the ground and finally wrenched the crumpled piece of paper from the boy's thick fingers.

"Paul! What are you doing? Give that back!"

"The name's Jonathan, Jonathan Murray, and don't you forget it!" And with that, he popped the small white piece of paper into his mouth and swallowed it.

"Nice job!" Shelley exclaimed as she held up her hand for a high five, only to suddenly slap it against her forehead. "We lost the Cookie Monster!"

"Come on, Shells, we stopped Jeffrey. That's pretty good for a couple of unexceptionals," Jonathan responded.

"I was so focused on this menace," Shelley

moaned, motioning toward Jeffrey, "that I completely forgot about him!"

"Well, not to worry, we didn't," a calm, self-assured voice said from behind Shelley. "We saw this strange man fleeing the playground, looking highly suspicious, so we thought it best to detain him."

Standing next to the slide, with Alan Feith in restraints, were Vera and Felix.

"Nice job," Shelley proclaimed.

"Right back at you," Vera responded.

OCTOBER 20, 9:56 P.M. THE LEAGUE OF UNEXCEPTIONAL CHILDREN HEADQUARTERS. WASHINGTON, DC

"You guys make a good team. Who knew exceptionals and unexceptionals could mix so well," Nurse Maidenkirk declared as Vera, Felix, Jonathan, and Shelley entered the conference room.

"The president's proud; he wanted me to thank you, to let each of you know that he'll never forget what you've done for this country," Hammett said while motioning for the kids to take a seat.

"What about Harold Foster?" Shelley asked. "Has he been arrested?"

"As it turns out, Jeffrey did this all on his own. He wanted the money so he could buy the Stradivarius cello from the Smithsonian. He thought it would make him the best cellist in the world," Nurse Maidenkirk explained.

"But how could Jeffrey have known the location of the president's safe unless his father told him?" Jonathan wondered aloud.

"Apparently, Harold Foster is a real chatterbox in his sleep," Hammett answered. "And once Jeffrey got his hands on the second code, he contacted his father's old friend Alan Feith, having realized that he would pay almost anything to access and then erase the Department of Justice's files on him."

"So no one wanted the nuclear codes," Felix confirmed.

"Not this time," Hammett said. "This time it was just about a greedy little kid and a greedy old man."

"So what happens now?" Shelley inquired. "Vera and Felix head back to old foggy-bottom England and you put us on another case?"

"No one calls it foggy-bottom England," Vera remarked.

"Well, they should," Jonathan mumbled.

"Normally, I'd put you through a proper course of training and then get you back out in the field as soon as possible," Hammett explained.

Shelley paused and then narrowed her eyes. "What do you mean by *normally*? What's abnormal about the situation? Did you finally realize that I'm exceptional?"

"Doll, you're an exceptional unexceptional, but an unexceptional nonetheless," Hammett replied, pushed back his chair, and then looked straight at Jonathan and Shelley. "Prime Minister Falcon spoke to President Arons this evening. He asked that both of you return to London with Vera and Felix. MI5 needs your help with a case."

"I'm sorry," Vera said, "but could you repeat that?"

"Hammett said we're going home with you," Shelley answered, and then broke into a massive smile. "Shells and Johno are about to shake up MI5."

OCTOBER 22, 9:32 A.M. 10 DOWNING STREET.
LONDON, ENGLAND

The man was thin and wiry. He wore a pristinely tailored navy suit and an expensive yet understated wristwatch. Stuck in a perpetual state of scowling, he was not exactly what Jonathan and Shelley expected of a prime minister, but then again they didn't have much of a frame of reference.

"President Arons informs me that you are the team responsible for stopping the sale of classified information, as well as bringing the vice president's kidnapper to justice," Prime Minister Falcon said in a stiff and formal manner befitting a conversation with the queen.

"To you he may be the vice president, but to me he's just Carl, a close personal friend," Shelley stated proudly while seated before the prime minister's desk.

"In the spirit of full disclosure, sir, I feel you should know that Shelley has an incredibly low bar for what constitutes a friend," Jonathan chimed in. "If you so much as wave at her, she'll consider you a bestie."

"But am I correct in assuming that you two were responsible for the success of the aforementioned mission?" Prime Minister Falcon pressed on.

"You are, sir," Jonathan confirmed.

"Good," the prime minister responded with a nod. "I do not ask for foreign aid easily. Only the most grave and dangerous of situations has brought me to do so today."

"PM, may I call you PM?"

"Please don't," Jonathan whispered to Shelley.

"You needn't worry because while my middle name isn't 'Grave and Dangerous,' it would be if it weren't illegal for minors to change their names without parental permission."

Prime Minister Falcon's stiff expression suddenly grew strained as he looked from Shelley to Jonathan expectantly.

"Oh, me?" Jonathan said. "I don't have a middle name, which is actually a good thing when you hear the ones my parents were considering... Flash, Boon, River... I mean, what were they thinking? I could never pull off any of those names."

"Yeah, no way. Frank or Larry maybe," Shelley added.

"I do not wish to offend you two, but—"

"Oh, it takes a lot to offend us, right, Johno?"

"Right. It's actually one of our strongest assets."

"You two seem terribly inept, rather shockingly so," Prime Minister Falcon declared unapologetically.

"Inept? You mean like we don't know what we're doing?" Shelley asked.

"Exactly," the prime minister answered.

"That's because we don't know what we're doing. And we're pretty much not good at anything," Jonathan explained.

"I hate to disagree with my partner, but I actually have quite a few hidden talents."

"She doesn't," Jonathan stated emphatically. "But what we do have is an ability to blend in, to go through life without showing up on anyone's radar. Why? Because we're average, forgettable, normal. In the words of Hammett Humphries, we live in the world's blind spot."

"And that blind spot gives us access to just about everything," Shelley said as she removed her glasses and looked the prime minister straight in the eye. "You may not believe it now, but in the end, you'll wish all your spies were as unexceptional as we are...."